THE SEVENTH TRUMPET

GABRIEL BLANCHARD

Clickworks Press

First publication: Clickworks Press, 2020

Release: CWP-GBSA1-INT-E.M-1.0

Sign up for updates, deals, and exclusive sneak peeks at clickworkspress.com/join.

Ebook ISBN: 978-1-943383-62-7

Paperback ISBN: 978-1-943383-63-4

CONTENTS

Liam H.

in memoriam

AUTHOR'S NOTE

This book contains a large proportion of dialogue in languages other than English, only some of which has been translated. Nothing essential to the plot of any story is concealed in the untranslated text; the use of other tongues is a thematic choice, not a puzzle. I am fluent in none of these languages, and, while I have taken what advice I could find from speakers and hope I have done my best with the translations, there are likely some errors all the same. To any native speakers who are annoyed by this, I apologize, and if I have the chance to release a corrected edition in the future when I have better information, I will be glad to do so.

And they said, Go to, let us build a city and a tower, whose top may reach unto heaven; and let us make a name, lest we be scattered abroad upon the face of the whole earth.

—Genesis 11.4

This, which is our first poem, might well be our last poem too. It might well be the last word as well as the first word spoken by man about his mortal lot, as seen by merely mortal vision. If the world becomes pagan and perishes, the last man left alive would do well to quote the Iliad *and die.*

—G. K. Chesterton, *The Everlasting Man*

A painter of the Umbrian school
*   Designed upon the gesso ground*
*   The nimbus of the baptized god.*
*   The wilderness is cracked and browned*

But through the water pale and thin
*   Still shine the unoffending feet,*
*   And there above the painter set*
*   The Father and the Paraclete.*

—T. S. Eliot, *Mr. Eliot's Sunday Morning Service*

SILENCE IN HEAVEN

In the beginning, the LORD created the heavens and the earth; and man he made in his own image. He placed man in a garden, to tend and to keep it. But man ate of a certain tree, the Tree of the Knowledge of Good and Evil, of which the LORD God had said to the man, *Thou shalt not eat of it; for in the day that thou eatest thereof thou shalt surely die.* And the LORD drave man forth from the garden, out into the silent earth, and he placed at the east of the garden Cherubins. And man was fruitful and multiplied, and his kind covered the face of the earth, and lived and died amid much toil, and all manner of sorrow.

Now it came to pass, after a great space of years, that the LORD visited men, coming among them with the form of a son of man, and spake unto them. And there were such as heeded the word of the LORD; but the greater part would not heed. And at times there was strife between them which would turn their hearts to the LORD their God, and them which would not, and often great misery and fear.

And again there was a great space of years, and men increased and grew wise. And they took thought, and crafted many subtle engines: such as would travel over land without horse or ox or any such thing, or upon the bottom of the sea, or among the clouds of heaven; and others, such as would send messages across many thousands of miles in the twinkling of an eye, or images likewise; and such engines as suffered man to traverse the æther and walk among the heavenly bodies; and divers weapons of war, which could waste whole cities in a single hour, and spread plagues, and strike death at great distances; and they trafficked in all manner of goods from every nation upon the face of the earth, gold and silver, silks and linens, luxurious foods, and the materials whereby the divers engines were fashioned. So they became great merchants, warriors, kings, and subtle men; and they took their pleasures as they would, and oppressed one another by their mighty craft, and heeded only such prophets as prophesied their desire. And the earth and the sea groaned under their dominion. But man was prosperous, and powerful, and exceeding wise in his own eyes.

Now it came to pass that the LORD God was grieved by the cruelties, the luxuries, and the manifold blasphemies of man. And having appointed in the secrecy of his counsel a time, for that he should judge them that dwell upon the face of the earth, he raised his hand: and the myriads of his holy ones, the Theotokos, the Seraphins, the Cherubins, the Thrones, the Dominations, the Virtues, the Powers, the Princedoms, the Archangels, the Angels, and all the multitude of Saints, ceased from their praises of him that sitteth upon the throne. And there was silence in heaven, for at the raising of his hand, every one of them became silent.

And the LORD stretched forth his hand to judge the earth: and the earth was judged.

GRANDFATHER SEER

The old man poked at the edge of the wadi with his stick. It was normal for it to be dry at this time of year, but this total withering of the grasses was strange. The trees, too, had an unhealthy look, and the wildebeest and gemsbok were lean and slow. The old man wondered mildly that the cheetahs were not glutting themselves on the easy meat, but he had seen no cheetahs for many days.

A hot breeze from the northeast rustled his robes. There had been many breezes of that kind of late: hot breezes bearing rain the color of tar, with a bad smell. He poked at the wadi again, more from habit than hope, clucked at his sheep, and wandered on.

The old man did not like to leave his cave often; it had taken him nearly a moon to chase out all the reptiles and insects that lived in its deeper recesses, and in his absence they would surely crawl back into their former haunts. Besides, he did not need to go down to the village often for extra food. It was easy enough to collect wild millet and dig up peanuts in the countryside, and his ewe gave him plenty of milk. But the villagers were superstitious—they revered him as a seer and a healer— and the strange rains and winds would surely have them in great anxiety. He felt vaguely responsible for their peace of mind.

He sang snatches of an old hymn as he walked, one that the Lutherans had translated into Swahili hundreds of years ago. The tune had an exotic brightness that he liked; it made him think of the sunrise.

'Ukawe ndoto yangu, o bwana wa moyo wangu,
Hayakuwa kuwa yote kwangu, kuokoa kwanga wewe ni,
Nawe mawazo yangu bora kwa siku au kwa usiku,
Uchao au kulala, uwepo wako mwanga yangu.'

A sandfly landed on the old man's shoulder, and he flicked it off. The persevering hum of its brothers was unusually loud. Unless that were only because of the unusual silence of the birds.

The sheep bleated at him moodily. She was hungry. The old man nodded, heading over to a tree—its bark was mottled and its foliage looked burnt—and sitting down in the shade. He unslung the water skin from his back, took a gulp, and then poured a little into his hand and extended it to the sheep. She drank, and then looked at him expectantly as he extracted a little millet from his pouch. The sheep munched, and then laid down, her face still slightly peevish.

'*Tamaa*,' the old man chuckled, and scratched behind her ear with a leathery finger. Really she did not need the water or the food at all, not with her fatty tail, which sustained her like a camel's hump. At least, when foreigners learned about the sheep's tail that was what they always said, though the old man had never seen a camel, and was not quite sure what they even looked like. But he did not need much food either; he was accustomed to long fasts. And if Zank Nofele's people should be short of food, as they sometimes were, it was better to give extra to the ewe and then subsist more on her milk.

The shade and the wind lulled him as he sat, and he wanted to stop and sleep, but this was not a good place. The cheetahs and leopards would be very interested in both the old man and his sheep. He stood up, brushing earth from his robes. He clucked to the sheep again, and she gave him a resentful look as she heaved up onto her hooves. Smiling, he gave her a gentle swat, and she trotted forward.

He looked eastward again. There were thunderclouds on the horizon. The old man's eyes were still sharp as a kite's, and he noted the uncharacteristic darkness of the sheets of rain they were shedding. His sandaled feet printed egg-like shapes in the red dust, which were swiftly swept away by the breeze. It was still another hour's walk to Zank Nofele.

* **

The old man knew something was wrong, terribly wrong, as soon as the village came in sight. The cooking fires were unlit. The goats, the sheep, a few tame tsebras, and all the chickens were loose, and entirely unattended. No one was outside, and there was no sound of fighting or talking or singing. It could not have been a raid, for raiders would have stolen the livestock. Was the whole village bedridden?

He came to the home of Ilta, the widow who lived at the edge of the village, and knocked on her door. There was no answer. He called her name, but no one said anything. A goat wandered up to him, whining noisily, and he shooed it away. The old man pushed the door open and went inside the hut.

At first he thought that Ilta must not be there. The smell was foul, and she was a tidy woman; besides, there was an ugly buzzing of flies, and she tended a clutch of geckoes to get rid of insects. The hut was without windows. He fumbled for a lamp—there was none on the crate she used as a table. Everything seemed to be disarranged. As he moved further into the room, the scent of oil mingled with the rot, and he felt gingerly on the floor; sure enough, here were the broken remains of her lamp.

'Ilta?' he said again. '*Ou li nawa?*'

He found her bed. His fingers came upon a hand; it was cold. He felt for a pulse, but jerked his hand back at the sensation of small, moist things. Maggots. The air in the hut stirred again at his sudden movement, and a warm, unbearable reek enveloped him.

The old man bolted from the hut, falling onto his hands and knees outside, panting. After a few moments, he vomited. Sweat trickled into his eye.

Wiping his mouth on his sleeve, he slowly stood up again and found his stick. Leaving his ewe to munch on some of the seedling corn that grew near the edges of Ilta's hut, he proceeded through the remainder of Zank Nofele. Corpse upon corpse was concealed in the huts: children, women, and men. The old man called until he was hoarse, trying Oshiwambo, English, German, Kavango, even his native Swahili from half a continent away. No one answered.

The sun was setting as the old man sat down on a tree stump close to the edge of the village. The late day washed everything in the deep, bitter red of the *mwegea* flower. It was cold. Slowly, weakly, the old man began to cry. He put his face in his brown hands and bawled like an infant. One hundred and fifty-three people had lived in the village, and he had found none alive.

He tried to pray: '*Baba Yetu uliye mbinguni, jina lako litukuzwe; ufalme wako ufike, utakalo—*' but he could not finish the line. He tried again. '*Baba Yetu uliye mbinguni, jina—jina lako … Baba Yetu … uliye …*'

It was useless. The old man's agony was too great; he was not prepared to surrender it to God. It was God who suffered the foolish, sweet-natured villagers to be filled with maggots. He could not accept that Ilta and Marta,

Ontagookamati and Mustafa, Ndeshi and Hango should all be taken from him at once. It was evil.

By the time he had tired himself out with crying, the sun had sunk below the horizon, and even the dusk light was almost gone. There was thunder behind him. He had not forgotten the black rains, and did not know what they would do. Reluctantly, he felt his way toward a hut close to the center of the village, whose occupant had left it before dying—perhaps to help a neighbor— and which was therefore nearly free of the hideous and increasing smell. He cooed to his sheep and a few of the other animals, not wanting them all to be subject either to the suspicious weather or to roving predators, and got them into the hut and laid down on the packed earthen floor. His ewe nuzzled his ear, and soon fell asleep. The old man's aging body soon slept too. He neither dreamt nor stirred that night.

✷　✷✷

The old man woke suddenly only a few minutes after dawn. He had heard something. He might once have dismissed it as a dream, but he was canny. Sixty years dwelling alone with God had taught him to distinguish dreams and fantasies from reality with great subtlety. There was calm outside the hut, except for a voice: a solitary voice, wailing, like a child's. There was someone else in the village.

He got up, disturbing a few of the goats. His own

ewe slept soundly on. Picking his way over the crowded floor, the old man pushed the door open. The rain had gone not long ago, and the red earth was now turned to brown mud, smelling faintly like lye. He listened carefully. The voice was still calling, in Oshiwambo, repeating the same words over and over: '*Meme! Ohandi ehama! Penduka, Meme! Penduka!*'

Grabbing his stick from its place by the door, the old man hurried toward the voice. It was only forty meters or so from the empty hut he had adopted. He stumbled on a sharp stone, hoisted himself up again, and continued. Reaching the hut, he banged his stick against the door.

There was a sudden yelp, and the voice stopped. The old man waited for a few long moments; then he opened the door. '*Ino tila,*' he said soothingly into the dark. '*Walelepo.*'

'*Tatekulu?*'

Nearly all the children in the village had called the old man *grandfather*, but he recognized this one's voice now. Fanuel—it was an angelic name, according to legend. He was so named because his skin was pale, paler than a European, and his hair was yellowish white (a silly reason for it, the old man thought, but a nice name all the same). When he was born, a few of the villagers had suggested that he be exposed as a bad omen, but the elders had overruled them and Fanuel had been kept. That was three or four years ago, maybe; the old man could not remember exactly when; everything went by so quickly.

The boy asked him to wake his mother. The old man's eyes could hardly make anything out in the gloom, except the whitish shape of the boy. But he knew already that the boy's mother was dead.

'*Itule*,' he said. There was no purpose in trying to explain. The boy was too young. He put out a hand, repeating that they should go, and the boy took it and left the hut with him, naked and blinking in the sunshine.

They went back to the old man's hut together. He doffed his robe and put it on the boy, using a piece of twine to hitch it properly—Fanuel's skin was far too delicate to withstand the harsh sun they would endure as they walked. The old man himself would have to go bare-skinned, but he was very dark and did not worry about the sun. The wells outside were suspect, thanks to the black rains, but there were a few skins in the hut that, by God's grace, were still partly full. There was a sturdy knife as well, with a leather sheath and a piece of string that served as a belt. The old man took a small bag of dried corn and filled a second bag with peanuts, found a couple of roughly hewn bowls, and placed the boy and their food on a tsebra. There was no harness, but he was able to find a switch, so that the beast could at least be impelled to move as needed.

The boy asked where they were going.

'*Okokule unene*,' the old man told him.

'Aaye Meme?' No Mama?

'Aaye Meme.'

He roused his ewe from her slumber, and she stared balefully at him for a moment before getting up. He hustled her and the tsebra out of the hut, clucking to any of the other animals that would listen; a few more sheep followed with them, and the old man breathed a sigh of relief. They set off westward, along the road to Etosha. It could not be more than a few days before they encountered the next village, and he was hoping for a road or a river before then.

* **

The old man and the boy walked for two weeks without seeing another living soul. Three villages went by in which all the inhabitants were rotting. He always made Fanuel stay at the edge of the settlement with the animals while he investigated; he was able to refill the water-skins in the first two places, but there was nothing more to be had from them. When he came back, tired and aching, the boy would ask him, *'Oto kongo shike?'*

'Itule,' the old man would answer, and on they would go.

The old man tried to pray as they went. He could never get further than *'Baba Yetu'* any more in his native Swahili; he could manage a few more phrases if he prayed in Latin or German, before the full meaning of the phrases caught up to him and tied his tongue in a knot. The boy did not pray along, but sometimes he sang, imitating the plainsong that he had heard now and again, filling in the gaps in his memory by imagination. The result was a comical mixture of African, European, and nonsense words, but it was lovely nevertheless. The boy's voice was pure, sweet, and trilling, like a lark's song.

On the fifth day out, one of the three sheep that had consented to follow with them died. The old man had thought it looked sickly, and before long its wool had begun to fall off, as if it were leprous. When it dropped, he stopped them, and when he had determined that it was dead, he used the knife to take some skin from the animal and made himself a loincloth. Then they went on.

By the time they reached Etosha, the knot had descended from the tongue through the old man's throat and into his stomach. Had the whole countryside been emptied? The sheep were starting to get hungry and thirsty—all the water and food that he and the boy could spare had been going to the tsebra. What little water Etosha held was a blackish, salty sludge. But there were several aloe trees growing there, and the old man cut many leaves to sustain them, if and when the water ran out. The old man decided to turn south and follow the road toward Windhoek.

They walked. The struggling grasses gave way to naked sand. Once, far off the road, they saw the remains of a leopard, rotting beside the skeleton of what seemed to be a gemsbok; they noticed it because of the hiss of the flies that were breeding in the meat.

One night, a week after Etosha, they stopped a little north of Otjiwarongo. The old man could see the town from where they made camp, but they did not advance to it; the boy and the beasts were exhausted. They set up a camp, and the old man found a dead baobab tree, broke some branches from it, and built them a fire. They had seen no predators since the dead leopard, but it did not pay to take chances. It was completely clear that night—a rarity in these strange weeks—and the numberless stars winked at them, white and blue in the blackness, as Fanuel slept.

The old man could not sleep. He sat and stared at the fire. It waved long orange arms toward the sky, and periodically cracked the pockets that had preserved moisture to nourish the baobab.

'*Kwa nini, Baba Kalunga?*' he murmured. Father God said nothing. A jackal howled nearby: its cry was suddenly stifled in a yelp, and there was quiet. The old man stood up and peered out westward, where the cry had come from, and saw a pale and ghostly shape advancing toward them.

'Who are you?' called out the old man in English. The shape said nothing, and he tried again. '*Ongoye lye? Wer bist du?*'

The shape answered him unexpectedly in Swahili: '*Tazama, Babu Mwonaji, rangi farasi.*' *Behold, Grandfather Seer, a pale horse.*

The old man nodded. '*Hazari ba jioni, Mtu Farasi.*'

The shape came up to the fire. It was stark grey-white, whiter than a European, and thin, with a distended belly, and too many fingers. It was naked. It appeared to be of no sex, and if it had ever had hair, all of it had long since fallen out. The shape seated itself on the earth at the edge of the firelight, its long limbs and unblinking eyes making it look like a spider. It fixed its gaze on the boy.

'*Owa hala shike?*' the old man asked suspiciously, fingering his knife.

The shape smiled horribly, without looking away from the boy. '*Nawe.*' I want you.

The old man shivered. He had dealt with devils before during his fasts; they rarely manifested themselves so explicitly, but it did happen at times. They were liars, but the horror was that it could be difficult to divine just what they were lying about. They knew how to mix the truth with lies, so as to throw an adept off the scent. The question was, this devil having said he wanted the old man, was that a lie or a treacherous truth?

'*Nawe,*' the shape repeated. It suddenly leaned forward towards the boy, and the old man darted between them. The shape laughed a guttural laugh and was still.

'"Dry bones can harm no one",' it said in English in a sing-song voice. '"Co co rico, co co rico."'

'*Mwongo,*' the old man hissed.

'*Ndiyo. Baba Mwongo anataka Babu Mwonaji.*' It laughed again.

'*Nenda zako, shetani.*'

'*In qua potestate hæc facis,*' the shape replied in the holy language, '*et quis tibi dedit hanc potestatem?*'

The old man opened his mouth to pray, but he found himself still unable. His face crumpled. Fanuel stirred in his sleep, but did not wake. '*Unataka nini na mimi?*'

The shape put its many-fingered hands behind its head and stretched out its long legs, as if it could warm itself at the fire. '*Kuja na kuona, babu.*'

'*Hakuna.*'

The shape smiled its horrible smile. '*Mvulana atakuja.*' *The boy will come.*

'*Kamwe!*' the old man shouted. The boy started awake, crying. The old man turned and crouched beside him, gathering him up in his arms, and looked back in wrath at the pale shape—but it was gone.

They set out again before dawn that morning. The boy was so drowsy he could barely stay on the tsebra, but the old man would not stay another moment in that desolate place; he wanted to get to Otjiwarongo and take refuge in the church there, where the devil would not follow. He could not forget its hungry eyes, and the jagged teeth it exposed whenever it looked towards the boy.

As they drew close to the town, close to sunrise, it became clear that whatever disaster had struck the villages had struck this place too. Every building was deserted; some were boarded up. The large hospital was not, and the old man found that, though the taps were no longer working, there was still a good deal of water in various kinds of containers, and even a little unspoilt food. The boy wanted to stay there when night came, but the old man refused.

They walked into the center of the town. It was noon. Newspapers were blowing around in the hot wind. Most of them were in Afrikaans, which the old man did not know. He spotted a broken metal box with English newspapers inside, and went up to it, prying it open with his hands, and wincing when he gave himself a long but shallow cut across his palm. He pulled out a paper and read the headlines.

Nuclear Warhead Detonated over Cape Town
No Leads in Assassination of Prime Minister
Pakistan Refuses Ceasefire with India
Kenya Announces Second Nuclear Test
British Ambassador Lynched in Erbil

A familiar rasping laugh caused the old man to look around sharply. No one was in sight except the boy and the animals. He tossed the paper away and took the boy's hand quickly. *'Itule.'* They made for the Catholic chapel at the edge of the town.

Sankt Josef had been boarded up, but the old man used the blade of the knife to extract the nails from some of the planks that barred the side door, and lifted the boy through the gap. He left the animals outside, taking the piece of twine he had used to truss up his robes for the boy, and tying it around their necks; they could break it easily if they were frightened by a predator, but they were tame enough to submit to it otherwise. Then he climbed into the hole himself.

The chapel was dim. Even the sanctuary lamp was unlit. Some light filtered in through the stained glass windows, but there were not many of them, and one had been boarded up—a few fragments of bright blue glass lay at its foot. The empty tabernacle stood gaping at the rear of the church.

The boy seemed quite happy. He flitted about in the gloom, a little white shape singing in a strange pidgin:

'*Ave Maria, uiaddi ongalasa Kalunga epuve,*

Gebenedeit unenepuve likaddi avese,

Et no mona die loie gebenedeit Yesu.'

He did not seem to know the rest of the Hail Mary. The old man smiled at him. He looked up at the altar again, and beside it he saw a statue of St Joseph holding the Holy Child. Or at least, it had been: the Child's head had been broken off, and so had Joseph's left arm. The old man stood up from his place and went over to the statue, and found the Child's head lying on the floor close by, but no sign of the patriarch's arm. Never mind. He picked up the head, kissed it, and gently set it in its proper place on the statue. If it were not disturbed, it would stay there.

The old man went back to his seat, releasing a sigh as he lowered himself into it. Fanuel ran up to him, his rose-pink eyes glowing.

'*Oto Meme?*'

He answered, '*Kombada.*'

'*Omuwa,*' the boy said brightly, and ran off again.

The day went on. He went to the hole at the side door, climbed out, milked his ewe for their supper, and climbed back in, and they ate. Night came, and the church was as dark as tar. The old man found matches to light some of the votives that remained—the candlesticks were too heavy for him to lift, and far too large for the boy. He makeshifted them bedding out of some of the worn-out vestments that had been left behind, and laid out a few cushions that had been placed on pews and prie-dieux, to serve as pallets. He placed them in the sanctuary, between the tabernacle and the altar. The Blessed Sacrament was not there, but it felt better to stay close to where It had been. The old man wondered whether he had grown a little superstitious himself.

He put out the candles, and they knelt to pray before sleeping. The boy said an Our Father, in his garbled version of Oshiwambo blended with German and Latin. The old man essayed to pray, and once more he could say no more than '*Baba Yetu.*' It had been discouraging before; now he was beginning to become angry. He had endured dryness and silence on his own behalf, but now, while that devil stalked them outside, hungry for the boy's soul? It seemed unjust and heartless. '*Nisaidie*,' he whispered into the dark.

'*Ou li nawa, Tatekulu?*' the boy asked him.

'*Ee.*' They laid down. The boy fell asleep quickly. The old man lay wakeful for some time, alternately nursing his bitterness and trying to subdue it; finally he also slept.

* * *

The old man was roused from his sleep by the sound of the church bell striking three. Someone else was here. The priest, maybe?

He leapt up. Something was wrong. The chapel was full of a dim, orange light, like a low fire, but none of the candles were lit. He looked at the boy; Fanuel was sleeping soundly. The old man walked slowly through the chapel, looking right and left for any sign of entry. He poked his head out of the hole: the sheep and the tsebra were slumbering complacently. He drew himself back in. The unaccountable light disturbed him.

'*Babu Mwonaji*,' came a deep, mocking voice from one of the doorways. It led to the bell tower.

'*Shetani*,' the old man growled. He made for the black opening.

The staircase twisted up the narrow bell tower; its wrought iron steps shivered beneath his feet as he climbed. At the top there was a trap-door in the floor of the belfry. The old man hoisted himself through, and found the pale shape standing by the bell-pull, leering at him.

'*Hazari ba jioni*,' it said.

'*Nenda zako*.'

'No. *Nakutaka*.'

'*Imperet tibi Dominus*,' the old man quoted. '*Vade retro*.'

The shape mockingly asked him why he did not say the exorcism in his native Swahili. The old man's face burned.

'*Hii ni kanisa*,' he insisted. '*Wewe hawana nafasi hapa*.' *You have no place here.*

The shape looked up dreamily and spoke from the old version of Job: '*Quadam autem die cum venissent filii Dei ut adsisterent coram Domino, adfuit inter eos etiam Satan. Cui dixit Dominus: Unde venis? Qui respondens aït: Circuivi terram et perambulavi eam*.'

The old man pleaded with him not to harm the boy. '*Hana hatia*.'

'*Mimi? I madhara mvulana?*' the pale shape asked in an indignant voice. '*Tena: Tolle filium tuum unigenitum quem diligis Isaac, atque offer eum holocaustum ...*' The words resounded in the old man's brain: *Take thou thy son, thine only son Isaac, whom thou lovest, and offer him for a burnt offering ...* He shivered.

The shape went past him and opened the trap-door. '*Hakuna*,' the old man cried, but it had already slipped down into the pitch-black hole. He followed as quickly as he could, tendons standing out from his wrists as he made his way, utterly blind.

He got down to the main floor; the fiery glow was still there. *'Fanuel? Ongaipe?'*

'Yeye hawezi kusikia wewe, Babu Mwonaji,' said the shape. *'Yeye ni usingizi.'*

The old man looked around, his eyes adjusting to the strange light. The white form of the boy was there, beneath the empty tabernacle, fast asleep as the devil had said. The pale shape was perched on the old man's own bedding, its knees drawn up by its ears and its gangrel arms wrapped about its shins. It was staring unblinkingly at the boy, with an expression almost of patience. It spoke meditatively.

'Upweke wa dunia. Wewe alikutana mapepo mengi katika jangwa. Atakutana nao wote, na wakati kufa, hakutakuwa na mtu wa kumlinda.' *The loneliness of the world. You met many demons in the desert. He will meet them all, and when you die, there will be no one to protect him.*

The pale shape looked over at him, and grinned again. The thing's face was an obscenity: the mouth was a sore, rotting until it fell open under its own weight. *'Kwa nini Baba Yetu kuokoa hii moja?'*

'Baba Yetu,' the old man whispered. No more words would come.

'Mtakufa, Babu Mwonaji, naye atakuwa mateka wa shetani.' *You will die, Grandfather Seer, and he will be the prey of the devil.*

'Hana hatia.'

'*Kutokuwa na hatia kamwe anakaa,*' the shape said calmly.

It turned away from the old man and contemplated the boy again. It never blinked. The old man advanced and sat down in front of the boy, setting his face toward the devil.

'*Humwezi kumwokoa,*' it said: *You can't save him.*

That, the old man retorted, was all the devil knew.

He broke a long splinter from his stick. Whenever his eyes began to droop, he found a sensitive patch of skin and drove the splinter into it, hard. The pale shape goggled and grinned, but neither it nor the old man moved from their places all the rest of that night.

A little light spilled through the windows at dawn. The boy stirred and groaned, and the old man turned to lay a hand on him. When he turned back, the pale shape had gone. The old man was not fooled. He had learnt in the desert that the devils almost never tormented a man continuously. If they did, he would become insensible to the temptation, as to a noise or a bad smell; they preferred to seem to go, and then come again later on. They truly vanished when they were truly defeated—not before.

But the shape would be gone for some little time. That was the way of things. The old man stood up, stretching his aching limbs, and went back to the broken side door to milk the ewe for their breakfast.

He found the ewe munching on some straggling grasses that had pushed their way up between the edges of the paving stones around the door. It gave him a glance and continued with its breakfast as he got down on his lean and calloused knees and began to milk it. The sun was shining.

Having filled up the two bowls, the old man carefully took them back into Sankt Josef. He came into the nave, but did not see the boy. *'Fanuel?'*

The boy came barrelling out of a door. *'Tatekulu!'* He leapt upon the old man with a hug, and the milk sloshed in the bowls.

'Hai ti!' cried the old man, laughing. *'Walelepo.'*

'Onda fya ondjala.' He reached out and took the carved bowl in his two small, white hands, and drank. *'Tangi,'* he said, and handed the bowl back and ran off the way he had come. The old man saw that it passed the door to the spiral staircase of the bell tower. His pale grey eyebrows drew together, and he sat down in the sanctuary and slowly drank his milk, thinking and listening.

After he had finished, drowsiness suddenly overtook him. He set his emptied bowl down, crawled over to the pallet he had made for himself, and slept.

But this time, while the old man slept, he had a dream.

✴ ✴✴

The old man knew somehow that it was the distant future—twenty years or more. He saw the boy, now a man, walking through the Kalahari with a heavy staff, in a traditional thin kilt and a broad-brimmed hat, rather like an old-fashioned priest's hat. It seemed to be early morning; the light was rosy, and the sky was dark blue, with a few stars in it.

The young man advanced up a hill. There was a single tree at the top of it, or the corpse of one; the old man could see the pale shape beside it, waiting for the young man. But, at the same time that he saw the pale shape, the old man could see it in the form of a beautiful young woman, and with the percipience of dreams he knew that she was the only thing the young man saw. She was lithe and shapely, and wore a skirt of rich, coral-pink silk, with a belt made of leopard skin; her breasts were uncovered.

Fanuel reached the top, and smiled at her. The shape smiled back, and came and began to undress him. The old man cried out to the young man, telling him to stop, that it was a falsehood and a sin, but there was no sign that he could hear him. But the pale thing did. Though its feminine simulacrum continued its play, at the same time, the shape looked over to the old man and whispered, '*Umekufa sasa. Yeye dhambi daima; sisi kuwa naye.*' *You are dead now. He sins continually; we have him.*

The old man turned away with tears, and sat down

and put his hands over his ears. It was no use. The animal grunts and cries of the young man and the succubus refused to be muffled.

At last, the unnatural pair finished. The young man stood up, pulling on his kilt and hat again. The succubus cooed to him, asking him to stay, but he refused. She said something the old man did not quite hear, though he did catch the word *okaana*. The young man answered her more harshly, and she began to weep and beg him to stay, insisting that she could feel the child growing. She caught the edge of his kilt. He spun around and struck her in the face with his staff. The succubus fell to the ground, mimicking tears and blood, and the young man strode off, cursing her; the pale shape laughed at the old man's look of horror. '*Yeye hajui,*' it told him.

'*Najua,*' replied the old man. '*Angalau* no *mtoto, Baba Mwongo.*'

'*Hakuna mtoto, hakuna. Hakuna wasio na hatia kijana mdogo.*' *No child, no. No innocent little boy.* The old man turned on the shape, burning with hatred; it was staring after the departing young man, looking almost wistful. '*Tutakwenda juu ya?*'

The old man looked up into the heavens. They were dark. '*Ndiyo.*'

They proceeded, following Fanuel, who was travelling to the south and a little westwards. '*Mbali na Jerusalem na Roma, unaelewa.*' *Away from Jerusalem and Rome, you see.*

'*Nyamaza.*'

'*Umefadhaika, Babu Mwonaji?*' said the shape. The old man did not answer this time.

In the manner of dreams, they were swept somehow to a new place, and it was later. The young man was in the ruins of a city now, in daylight, and the pale shape had departed from the old man's side. Now it had taken the form of a fellow young man, European in descent, also kilted and with a lion skin around his shoulders. He was sitting in a gutted building—it had perhaps been a hospital—sharpening a crude knife, and looking at a faded photograph that he had taken from a pouch at his waist. He looked up at Fanuel as he entered, and leapt to his feet with a bellow of fear. '*Ein Gespenst!*'

'No,' said Fanuel in thickly accented English, 'only an albino.'

He looked around the ruins. The simulacrum-man remained tensed, his eyes following the other's movements warily. Fanuel looked back at the simulacrum. 'This picture, it is of whom?'

'*Meine Tochter,*' said the simulacrum. Evidently it understood English, but did not speak it, or pretended not to. '*Sie ist tot.*' The pale shape that coinhered with the phantasm looked over to the old man and winked at him.

'Radiation sickness?' asked the young man, but the simulacrum said nothing. Fanuel picked up the photograph and looked at it. 'I want your knife. Give to me.'

The simulacrum was bewildered. '*Abe ich brauche es. Ich habe es gemacht.*'

Fanuel smiled. It was not a nice smile. He stepped back a little from the simulacrum-man, his hat shading his face, and raised the photograph as if to tear it in two.

The simulacrum leapt forward with a cry. '*Nein! Nein! Nehmen Sie das Messer, ich will es nicht!*'

Fanuel stepped well back, still holding the photograph. He tore into it a little, close to the pretty, smiling girl's eye. '*Nein! Bitte!*' He picked up his knife by the blade, nodded deliberately at Fanuel, and set it down on the dirt-strewn floor within his reach. The young man picked it up, examining it with a satisfied expression.

The simulacrum looked anxiously at him. '*Kann ich mein Foto haben zurück, bitte, Herr?*'

Fanuel looked at him, tucking the knife into the waist of his kilt. Then he smiled nastily again, and ripped the photograph right through.

'*Nein! Nicht bitte, nicht!*' The simulacrum pleaded with him to stop, but the young man tore it into quarters, and then eighths, and continued, until the photograph was no more than a handful of garbage. The simulacrum fell to its knees, weeping uncontrollably, and Fanuel dusted off his hands over it, showering it with fragments of paper. He pulled the lion skin from the simulacrum's shoulders; it did not even try to protest. Then he turned and continued walking, whistling brightly.

'*Sisi kuwa naye,*' repeated the pale shape. The simulacrum dissolved around it; the sounding of crying faded the most slowly, giving an ugly contrast to the young man's whistling. '*Lakini unastahili kutambua.*'

'*Mimi!*' said the old man.

'*Wewe naendelea naye hai,*' the pale shape explained. '*Vinginevyo sisi kamwe inaweza kuwa kupotoshwa yake.*' *You kept him alive. Otherwise we could never have deceived him.*

'*Nyamaza!*'

The shape shrugged and told him to come along, that there was still more to see. He began to follow in the footprints of the young man; again the old man followed after him, burning with wrath, determined not to let the devil fulfill its diseased plan to corrupt the boy.

Place and time shifted again. They were near the shore of the sea, and it was a red evening. Fanuel was sitting on the crest of a low dune, looking out over the water. He was very lean now, and his hair had gone from pale yellow to pure white. The old man looked around, but he saw the shape nowhere.

'*Fanuel?*' he said. There was no response. He tried speaking louder, he tried different languages, he tried waving his hand in front of the young man, he even tried smacking him. Nothing.

He sat beside him on the sand and looked out. Then he noticed a strange disturbance on the surface of the water. The old man leaned forward. It was bubbling.

Out of it came the pale shape. The young man started. Apparently he could see it this time. Its head was in the shape of a hyena's, and its skin seemed to be scaly and dried, like a crocodile's. It emerged from the water completely erect, without any suggestion of swim-ming; though its mouth did not move, its voice said to the old man (and he intuited that he alone could hear the words of the Apocalypse, heralding the beast from the sea), '*Vidi de mare bestiam ascendentem, et dedit illi draco virtutem suam.*'

'*Olye oo?*' called Fanuel to the shape.

'*Aame xo Satana,*' it said: *I am your father the Devil.*

The young man rose and went down to the shore to meet it. It advanced from the seawater and stepped onto the wet sand, face to face with Fanuel.

The old man could neither rise and walk down to them, nor look away. He could not hear them over the crashing of the waves; the tide was coming in, and they were speaking in low voices. The hyena shape seemed to be urging something upon the young man, and he was pondering whatever it was. The young man took a step back, at which the old man sighed with deep relief. He stood up and drew closer to the conversing pair.

'*Tala,*' said the shape, and turned to face the sea. It swept its hands upward.

There was a great noise, like thunder and rain, and a gigantic form emerged out of the water. Or no—it was a shape that was fashioned out of seawater, held in its form by some invisible force. It was a duplicate of the pale thing conversing with the young man, like an Egyptian god, and it followed its master's movements perfectly. The shape moved to the left, and the sea giant moved to the left; the shape squatted, the sea giant squatted; the shape gestured over its head, the sea giant did the same.

'*Ti paife*,' the pale thing said. The young man nodded. He strode further forward, till one foot was in the ocean and one on dry land, and looked straight upward, his grey-white skin looking bloody in the setting sun. He raised his hands in an obscene gesture and began to scream blasphemies at the top of his voice.

The old man sat down suddenly. The coarse, damp sand yielded to him. He stared at the young man, barely seeing him, overwhelmed by the sound of his voice.

The pale shape spoke to the old man again, quoting: '*Illi hæc eo omnia dabo quia cadens adoravit me.*' *All these things will I give thee, if thou wilt fall down and worship me.*

'*Huenda mungu akukemee.*' *May God rebuke you.*

'*Ambayo si kumsaidia—si kwamba hivyo?*' *That won't help him—isn't that so?*

The old man laid down on the sand, face down, and wept. There was no strength in him any more. Even when Fanuel came over, still blaspheming, and began to strike him, the old man could neither move nor cease from weeping. The blows became harsher, the voice became louder, but the old man's deepest agony was for the boy's damnation. He had failed him. Or, he would fail him—it made no difference whether it was phrased as past or future; the fact of his failure blazed within him, consuming him.

✳   ✳✳

At last, Fanuel succeeded in waking the old man up.

He had been shaking him more and more vigorously for several minutes, saying '*Tatekulu! Tatekulu!*'

The old man started as he woke, and sat up quickly, grabbing the boy's arm tightly. The boy yelped, more from being startled than from pain. All the lights and shadows were different. The old man looked around; it must be mid-afternoon, or later.

The boy asked about dinner. The old man nodded and said something, he didn't know what, and went to milk the sheep.

Outside, the sun was sinking through the air, boiling it. He sat down by the ewe, placing the first bowl underneath its udder, and began to milk. The steady, familiar motion was reassuring: pull, pull, pull, pull, and the milk flowed and frothed in the wooden bowl. Then in the second bowl, just the same way: pull, pull, pull, pull. The tsebra woke from its late afternoon nap—being tied up bored it terribly, but the old man did not know what else to do with it. He went through the square before the church, methodically searching for the straggling weeds they would eat. He pulled up what he could find and brought them back to the animals. It was not really enough, but it would have to do for the present, until the old man determined where to go next. Whenever, wherever, that was.

He went back inside with the bowls of milk and handed one to the boy. Fanuel took it, cheery and forgetful, and quickly drank it and began to run about the gloomy chapel again.

The old man sat, hardly seeing him, thinking. After a few minutes, he called to the boy.

'*Koshawa?*' he asked. The boy looked blankly at him; remembering his garbled Hail Mary, he tried again. '*Baptizus es? Bist du getauft?*'

'*Ee, Tatekulu,*' said the boy.

'*Nawa.*' He nodded and continued to think.

'*Olye penya?*'

The old man looked up. The boy was pointing to the yawning dark of the bell-tower's door. His heart contracted, and he quickly lied that there was nothing up there.

'*Onda udite ou,*' he insisted: *I hear someone.*

'*Aaye, ahowe,*' said the old man repressively. The boy did not look altogether satisfied, but he resumed his strange game before long.

The sun set; the old man lit candles and they burned low and began to go out; he put Fanuel to bed. He decided, as the boy fell asleep, that moving on the next morning would be best. There were clearly no other survivors in Otjiwarongo, and the next logical place to look was Windhoek. If that too proved desolate, he was unsure what to do afterward. Go to the seashore, perhaps, and follow the coast southwards, on the off-chance that South Africa had been spared the worst. Or the other direction, towards the jungles in northern Angola and Cameroon, where animals and plants were far more plentiful, and surviving comestibles were therefore likely to be less scarce. Trying to return eastwards, to his native country, would be difficult at the best of times, on account of the mountains; he would certainly not try it now.

The hours passed. He got up and extinguished the few candles he had left lit, and went to his pallet. He was unsettled by the absolute silence of the night. The faint hum of termites, dung beetles, and sandflies had been an ignored and familiar backdrop to the old man's whole life: he could hear none of them now.

Some time past midnight, he still had not succeeded in falling asleep. He sat up, wiping a little sweat from his forehead. The church was still cool and dark; the weird phosphorescence of the previous night was safely absent.

'*Babu Mwonaji*,' came the voice of the pale shape out of the bell-tower doorway. Immediately he turned his face away from it in a gesture of refusal. He wasted no words on it. The call was not repeated.

Nonetheless, after a short time, the old man stood up and began to tread quietly about the church. He looked over at the boy several times, from differing angles. The boy slept with an astounding peacefulness: his brows, his lips, his fingers, all seemed to express complete, contented rest. Hardly anyone was capable of such innocent sleep. Worry, guilt, spiritual conflict, exhaustion itself, rendered slumber a strangely complicated thing for adults.

He had made two full paces of Sankt Josef before he noticed the whispering. Since he had been trying to put the thought of the pale shape from his mind, he had not been attending to the absence or presence of its voice; but he could hear it now, soft and yet distinct, like the sound of a cheetah's claw being dragged across stone.

The old man was directly opposite the door to the bell-tower. He approached the empty arch, but he saw and heard nothing beyond it. The voice was somewhere else, somewhere in the body of the church—he realized it when he heard the whispering again, behind him.

'*Fanuel,*' it was saying, '*okaana kange. Aame xo.*'

'*Mwongo!*' hissed the old man, and started back toward the boy. He was still asleep, but his sleep had become restless: he tossed and whimpered and sighed on the cushions. The old man saw the faintest glimmer of eyes, in the dark above the boy, and a shudder ran through his body. The shape was in the sanctuary itself.

He reached the sanctuary and fell on his knees before the empty tabernacle, beside the boy, his hand outstretched, as if he could swat the devil away like a sandfly. '*Baba Yetu uliye mbinguni, jina lako … litukuzwe; ufalme … wako ufike, utakalo …*' He stumbled hastily through the first part of the Our Father, hoping he could recite the whole prayer before his desolation caught up with him; he found the words deserting him, tried again, tried again. '*Baba …*' The old man's voice was reduced to a rasp, and finally to silence.

The emptiness of the night heavens pressed down upon his brain. He was cold.

'*Okaana kange,*' the shape murmured gently.

The old man decided, and moved. His own pallet

had been made of cushions and a surplice, rolled up to serve as a pillow. He picked up the surplice and stepped softly over to the boy and kissed his forehead. He prayed desperately that the boy would not stir: '*Baba, tafadhali wala kumwamsha.*'

The glimmering eyes of the devil stayed above the boy's form as the old man pressed downward. It did not take long: the fabric was dense, and the old man made tight folds with it. When it was over, the eyes seemed to blink and fade, and a soft laughter rippled through the air of the chapel, like the noise of a putrefying animal's carcass collapsing on itself.

'*Nawe,*' the shape whispered one last time.

Suddenly, with a quick shock of pain, the old man saw it all. '*Mwongo,*' he rasped again—*liar*—but without resentment. All of that energy was bent in upon himself.

The boy had never been in danger. Or if he had, that was not why the devil had come to the old man; why would it tip its hand that way? It had said truthfully, over and over, that it wanted him, never that it wanted Fanuel. All the rest had been false. And the old man had swallowed every word and picture, even in the midst of reminding himself that he was dealing with the Father of Lies.

'*Jesus, mwana wa David, nihurumie mwenya dhambi.*'

His tongue was loosened. The old man repeated the prayer for hours, till the dark fell over his eyes.

* **

In the morning the old man buried Fanuel's body.

It was curiously cool when he first went out. The sky was mottled with clouds, and there was a heaviness in the air; there would be thunder soon. The old man untied the tsebra and sent it on its way, but kept the sheep with him to tend them. They had made short work of the local weeds, so he pulled out a little more millet and gave it to them. Their eager lips tickled him.

The old man set down one of the wooden bowls beneath his ewe, and essayed to milk her, but somehow he could not lift his hands to her. She bleated at him, with a curious sweetness. He sat beside her for a few minutes, trying to make his hands milk her, but it was no use. At last he shrugged, put the bowl away, and stood up. '*Mimi itakuwa haki ya nyuma,*' he said to her, and scratched her nose.

He climbed back into the dark church. The white shape of the boy's body was faintly brightened—a little sunlight was falling in through one of the windows behind the altar. The old man looked at it for a time; the light moved; he stirred, and went to see if there was a shovel or a spade in one of the closets.

There was no shovel. He found a large, flat rock close by outside, and used it as a makeshift trowel. The earth near the chapel was dense, and he could manage no more than half a meter's depth before exhaustion overcame him. He rested for a short time. Again he could see black rains falling, out at the horizon. Probably they would reach Otjiwarongo in about three hours. Then he went in, took the boy's body in his arms, and laid it in the shallow grave as if in a cradle. Perhaps he had damned himself, but at least the boy …

He knelt at the graveside and traced crosses on the boy's forehead, lips, palms, soles, and breastbone. He could not remember the funeral rite proper, and anyhow he had only been ordained a deacon before retreating to the wilderness; but something should be said. He fumbled for a few moments, and rasped out a few lines from the sixty-eighth psalm—grossly inappropriate under the circumstances, but he couldn't think of anything else for some reason—and a Latin antiphon for the repose of the dead: '*Mwimbieni Mungu, lisifune jina lake, mtengenezeeni njia ya barabara, apitaye majangwani kana mpanda farasi; jina lake ni Yahu; shangilieni mbele zake. Baba wa yatima na mwamuzi wa wajane, Mungu katika kao lake takatifu. Ee Mungu, ulipotoka mbele ya watu wako, ulipopita nyikani; nchi ilitetemeka naam, mbingu zilidondoka usoni pa Mungu; hata Sinai usoni pa Mungu, Mungu wa Israeli. Requiem æternam dona eo Domine: et lux perpetua luceat eo.*'

His ewe wandered up to him and nuzzled his side. He laid a grateful hand on her head. Then, he shoved the dark red earth over the boy, forming a small mound above the grave and patting it down firmly. He found a pair of sticks and tied them into a rude cross with the piece of twine he had bound Fanuel's robe with, planting it at the boy's head. Then he got up and left the city, the sheep trailing behind him.

URIEL

In over two thousand years, nothing about the land had changed. Oh, the buildings had, and the people who owned them or fought over them; the weapons they fought with and the destruction they left behind had changed. Romans, Persians, Arabs, Egyptians, Turks, Englishmen, strange fair-skinned Jews, Americans, Arabs again, Russians, Americans again, Jews again. Villas and fora, gem-studded shrines to the new god, cupolated mosques tiled with gold and burning blue, the porticoes and pinnacles and fountains of the Ottomans, quiet green-lawned *qibbutzim*, sleek and ugly European-style skyscrapers, the curvaceous floral domes and enclosures of the Neo-Baroque—then, rather suddenly, piles upon piles of broken stone, metal, and glass, followed for a little while by the crude huts of a people who had lost the art; and then, the rotting of the huts, emptied of inhabitants, the hills of Shomron breezing with notes hardly above silence.

But the land itself was practically untouched. The date palms were a little the worse for wear, their broad leaves tinged with yellow; but they were still hale, like curmudgeonly old men with kind hearts. The anemones still winked up at the sky, the bold lilies towering above them. The wizened olives nodded to the palms, their twisted branches reaching out as if to clasp a hand in greeting. And the dappled pattern of grass and yellowish earth, as if all the hills and plains were a shore that had lost its sea, stretched out to the very horizon.

Uri looked out from the mountain over it all. Once upon a time, the sea itself would have been visible even from here, the one the Romans had called *Mare Nostrum* as if they owned the thing. The pollution of an age recently ended, giving way to God knew what æon, had obscured the air. But the dead cities that lay sleeping among the hills and wadis could still be picked out: Beyt Lechem, Yericho, Ramallah, Chevron, and the mother of them all, Yerushalayim. Even her broken walls sat queenlily upon the pinnacle of Har Tziyon. A little flash, like a meteor, came from her.

He sighed and rose from the rock he had been sitting on. He did not know why he was heading to the City; it had been centuries since he had understood why he went this way or that. A phrase from the new prophecies rose to his memory, rankling him: *Thou shalt stretch forth thy hands, and another shall gird thee, and carry thee whither thou wouldest not.* At any rate that part was true, whatever else the sorcerer had said or not said—or, Uri thought sourly, whatever else so many Jews had decided to fawn on him for. No respect for the Law, no firmness in resisting *mesithim.* He was sorry to see the city laid low—*Eykha yashvah vadhadh, ha'ir rabathi 'am haythah, k'almanah; rabathi vagoyim, šarathi vammdhinoth haythah, lamas*—but not as sorry as he might have been.

His sandalled feet progressed down the rough slope, nimbly avoiding the looser stones and deceitful patches of unsettled earth. His staff thudded regularly on the ground as he went. He had an idea that he knew what had caused the brief flash of light. He had not seen his irksome counterpart in some years, but it seemed fitting somehow that they should meet again now.

✳ ✳✳

It took about three days to descend from the mountaintops into the deep rift of the Yarden and up out of it again, to the edges of Yerushalayim. The hardship, and the time, were nothing to Uri in themselves: he had crossed everything from the Pyrenees to the Hindu Kush on foot. And the opportunity to bathe in the storied Yarden once more, even if its waters were lower and more muddied than the last time, was a pleasing thing. But the notion of his counterpart did tend to occupy his mind. He never quite felt that he knew what to do with his rival, mentally, though he knew well enough that he didn't need to decide much and didn't have the power to decide much.

A locust crossed his path as he waded up out of the Yarden, and he snatched it. He had not eaten in two days; most of the surviving animals were unclean. He needed uncommonly little, so it was not much of a trial to fast, but his palate and his stomach were grateful for the small nourishment all the same. As he broke open the muscular legs, the thin crack of the exoskeleton could be heard in the unnatural silence of the Yarden's aged valley. Birds and insects were almost all gone; even the water flowed quietly down to the arid south.

Uri climbed. The steep walls of the valley were greener than most places managed to be these days, but even so, the green had turned to grey in many places. He pushed his way up through the remnant of weeds and rushes, up into the plateau and then the lower parts of the hills proper, until the sun had set and the handful of visible stars winked at him. It was only the beginning of Shisshiy, so there was no need to be specially attentive to the sunset, but of course there would be tomorrow. Yet he would be in Yerushalayim long before then. He smiled as he found a flatter part of the slope, with a little more grass, and laid himself down to go to sleep. A Shabath spent in the Holy City was a rare pleasure; he had not tasted it in more than four hundred years.

★　★★

The meandering road up into the hills was dry and silent. A young vulture with copper-yellow wings and a slender white head watched Uri curiously. *'Ţerem,'* he said to it with an indulgent chuckle. *'B'qaruv, achi.'*

But soon or late, he hoped his counterpart would be first. And that he would be there to watch.

A keening whistle met his ears, as he knew it would. 'Och! Up 'ere, mate!'

'Ani,' he croaked, *'lo' chaver shelekh.'*

'Aye, that's what thou said'st in 1853,' called back the other voice merrily. 'An' 1993 an' 2063. Get thee a fresh tune, mate, that one's gone stale.'

'Mesith.'

'Christ-killer.'

'Goy.'

'That an insult, is it?'

'Prutzat kalbon.'

This was met with silence. Uri smiled grimly. Every victory was worthwhile, however small.

He heaved his way over a broken wall, pushing himself up with his stick. The dust of the crumbling stones left pale marks on his robe. He scraped his shin slightly. He rose to his feet, brushed some dirt from his front, and was promptly brained by a rock.

As the heavens spun above him and his ears rang, a face came shakily into his field of vision—the blonde, boyish, scowling face of his counterpart.

'Don't call an Irishman's dam an 'ore, mate, thou kenn'st that.'

He stretched a hand out to Uri, who took it with a groan, and helped him back onto his feet. The *goy* tossed aside the mirror he had been using to signal his counterpart; each had an intuitive sense of the other's presence, but not a very specific one. The two walked side by side for a while, from the outskirts into the trashed and broken remains of the Holy City.

'*Ha'am iysh mishehu le'khol?*' asked Uri.

'Here,' said his counterpart, without looking at him, passing him something wrapped in paper. He opened it. It was a handful of dried figs.

'*Zah hara'iyon shelekh shel vedhikhah, ani manikh?*'

'Och, leave off wi' the palaver an' set to,' the other replied.

The Jew shrugged, feeling a little guilty for his ungrateful response, and put a fig in his mouth. The Irishman smiled at him sidelong. 'Besides, 'tis a bonny joke, no?'

Uri glared at him and spat out the fig; his guilt had evaporated. He handed the remainder back to his counterpart.

'Suit thyself,' said the other with a shrug, and began to eat.

✱　✱✱

What was left of the Qubbat, as the Arabs had called it, was still impressive, even beautiful. Most of the gold on the dome had been stolen, in the earlier days of the collapse when gold was still worth having, but a little bit was left on the top, flashing brilliantly when the sun was out. The lapis-blue walls had proven more difficult to repurpose, so they didn't show much damage from looters, and the serpentine elegances of Arabic calligraphy could still be distinguished on most parts of the architraves.

It was far enough past noon that the Qubbat was casting a little shade on its east side, and the two men sat down there. A few surviving trees blocked their view of Har ha-Zeythim and the lower parts of the old Muslim quarter of the city, not that there was much of it left to see in any case.

'I ken thou speak'st perfect good English, Uri. Is there a reason—?'

'*Mah lo' b'sedher bizah?*'

'Only as my Hebrew ain't tip-top, as thou kenn'st right well.'

'*Atah ha'achadh sh'uhev ladbar*, Ciaran.'

'Och, forget it,' said his counterpart angrily. Uri smiled to himself. Nothing still gave him such pleasure as needling his opposite number, who had no business being around after sixteen centuries, and certainly not here of all places. Suddenly a curiosity entered his head, and he caught his tongue only just in time; he had already parted his lips to ask.

But Ciaran had noticed, and smiled at him. 'Well, go on then. Mate.'

His companion glowered as fiercely as he knew how. *'Lammah lo' Roma?'*

'I've already been to Rome. There's nothin'. Christ put the lights out when He left. Naught but some rubble, a lot o' dirty water, an' o' course the souvenir shop. They maun to have the souvenir shop, ken, even at the Last Day. Mark me words, Uri, there we'll be a-watchin' the Glory descend, an' a bit to its left there'll be a fat, painted cow trying to sell thee a commemorative mug o't.'

The other man laughed in spite of himself. The *goy* laughed too; then his smile faded and his face became darker. 'This is our last time, now. Don't think I nae ken it. Cannae explain it, I just know, somehow, it's the end … Nae more seven sevens an' all—'

'Ašer sheva'im,' Uri corrected him.

'Och, give over.' He looked at the last fig suspiciously, sniffed it, and threw it off the decaying wall that had once been the retainer of the Mount; it flew far over the rubble and the occasional clean-picked bone, and landed with a faint plop that could be heard clearly in the massive silence. 'Thou mindest that first time we met? Where was that, Paris?'

'Liyon.'

'Och aye, Lyons. Kent thou wast another one the moment I laid eyes on thee, an' I dare say thou kenn'st the same o' me.'

'Hen.'

'An' after that, what—Venice, Cairo, Kaifeng, New York, Prague … I cannae recall them all.'

'*Lo l'phiy hathaqanon, gam ken.*'

Ciaran smiled briefly, and then became grey-faced again, looking at his hands. 'Thinkest th'alt get taken up? Go to heaven an' all?'

'*Kamuvan. Ani Yehudhi.*'

The *goy* smiled sourly, and went for the jugular. 'So was Korah.'

Uri's face became black, and he stood up.

'Och, go on now,' said the other, 'it was only a bit o' fun …' But the Jew was already walking away. 'Uri! I'll say sorry if it please thee!'

'*Me'ochar. Makhar ha-Shabath,*' he called back.

'The sun winnae set for hours!'

'*Me'ochar.*'

✶　✶✶

The evening was cool, and unexpectedly clear. A wind had come out of the southwest, disrupting the suffocating coverlet that usually lay atop the air. The stars would be out tonight.

There was a ghastly, metallic screeching in the distance that made Uri start, but then he realized it was vultures. Probably they had found the carcass of some hardy animal that had finally succumbed to its own hunger.

The setting sun was concealed behind a cloudbank, but Venus was hovering over it. Uri closed his eyes and began to recite, the opening stars serving for his candles:

'Barukh atah ha-Shem Eloheynu, melekh ha'olam, asher qidishanu b'mitzvotayv vetzivanu l'hadhliq ner shel Shabath. Amen. Vay'hiy 'erev vay'hiy voqer, yom ha-shisshiy. Vay'khollu ha-shamayim veha'aretz, vekhol tzeva'am: vay'khal Elohiym baiyom ha-shevi'iy m'lakhtho asher 'ašah, vaiyishboth baiyom ha-shevi'iy ...' Blessed art thou (the Name) O God, king of all, who hast hallowed us with His commandments and hast commanded us to light the lights of Shabath. Amen. And there was evening and there was morning, the sixth day. And the heavens and the earth were finished, and all the host of them: and on the seventh day God finished His work that He had done, and He rested on the seventh day ...*

His prayer was interrupted by another shriek. Why did the Lord create vultures, he wondered irritably. *'Mikal m'lakhtho asher 'ašah,'* he continued firmly. *'Vay'varekh Elohiym eth yom ha-shevi'iy —'*

Another screech, followed by a human yell. Uri opened his eyes and sat up, looking down from his bivouac on the slope of Har ha-Zeythim with mounting annoyance. The other one knew perfectly well he'd be praying now. He peered toward the Qubbat; there was some sort of commotion, though it was hard to distinguish through the trees. Then, he heard a different sound, neither human nor avian: a shrill, canine howl.

Wolves.

Uri was running down the slope before he realized he had risen. His foot thudded wrongly against a stone: he stumbled and twisted his ankle, then immediately got up and ran again, ignoring the screams of protest his tendons sent to his brain. There had been no wolves in Yehudhah for centuries, he thought to himself; the easy pickings among the dead must have lured them back, that and the absence of hunters. A single adult grey wolf could weigh nearly as much as a small man; the other one was—well, not *so* small, but small enough, and anyhow wolves didn't hunt alone. Uri leapt over a fallen tree and began racing up the crumbled steps that led toward the top of Har ha-Bayith, straining his ears for any sounds from above.

He jumped over the last two steps, wincing as he landed on his sprained ankle, and swept over to his right. Ciaran was holding a burning brand from his little fire, trying to fend off five slavering wolves, swishing the branch this way and that till the old Jew was impressed he hadn't hurt himself with it yet.

Uri picked up a broken piece of masonry and hurled it at one of the wolves. It missed narrowly, and the wolf leapt back with a snarl; they had been alerted to his presence. He rushed at them, and one of them jumped toward him. He leapt aside and grabbed another rock. The wolf landed just past him, and he flung it as hard as he could at the beast. This one struck true, right in the wolf's eye, and it dropped to the ground, dead. A squeal of pain came from another as Ciaran finally landed a hit on its snout with his torch, and it ran away, with two more of its companions. But the last and largest of the wolves was more stubborn than the rest: it crouched at the edge of the firelight, growling and salivating at the two men. This one was hungry.

Ciaran moved to his left, brandishing his flaming stick. Uri gradually drew closer, glancing around for another useful stone. A snarl and a bellow of pain made him whip his head back up; mindless of the fire, the gigantic wolf had jumped on the Irishman, knocking his weapon from his hand, and was now snapping at his neck. Ciaran was barely managing to avoid the beast's assaults, and was getting his forearms torn open by its teeth.

A bark of surprise turned into another fury of snarling, and Ciaran was free. He pushed himself up, earth and blood caking his hands, and looked wildly around for the wolf. Despite having no weapon, Uri had rammed the thing off of him and was now wrestling it, his teeth bared, making no noise except hard, steady breathing. He seemed to be trying to maneuver his hands toward the animal's face, perhaps to put his thumbs through its eyes, but its fangs and claws were swiping at him and he couldn't reach.

Ciaran looked around. He didn't want to take another brand from the fire, for fear of hitting Uri with it rather than the wolf. He spotted a large, angular rock close at hand, sprinted over to it, and came back to the man and the beast, who were both lying on the ground. With a tremendous yell, he smashed the wolf's head with the rock, which broke in half.

The threat dealt with, Ciaran collapsed onto the

ground. The night seemed extremely cold all of a sudden; he edged toward the fire without standing up. The two men panted together for a few minutes.

'*Ha-ze'ev hayah meth kvar, atah yudh'a,*' said the Jew at last.

He looked over. It was hard to tell in the hideous mass of pink and red at the wolf's head, but it did look as though Uri might have reached the eyes while he was off finding a stone.

'Bastard,' he panted, 'ye might hae said.'

'*Ani mitzṭa'ar,*' said the other.

Ciaran began laughing weakly; Uri followed with faint gasps. The humming of beetles and the quiet pops and cracklings of the fire nearly hid the sound.

✶　✶✶

'Th'art wounded,' said Ciaran after a long silence.

'*Hen. Ha-ze'evim …*'

'I ken.' He pushed himself up from the ground again. 'There must be somethin' about as we can make into bandages.'

'*Lamah?*'

The other one blinked. 'Because th'art wounded. I'll not hae thee bleed to death before me, not after savin' me skin.'

'*Amen, omer ani lakhem,*' answered Uri bitterly, '*kiy yesh ba'omdhim poh ašer l'yiṭe'amu ṭa'am miythah 'adh kiy-yir'u eth-Ben-ha-Adham ba bemalkh'utho.*'

'What does that mean?'

'*Lo goses*,' he rasped: *I'm not dying*.

Ciaran ignored his companion's sour confidence, and wandered around the Qubbat for a while, looking for something to stanch wounds with. His own hæmorrhaging arms went ignored, until he stumbled back to the firelit circle, his face white, a bunch of leaves and old pieces of vine in his arms. Uri looked up at him, then spoke sharply. '*Mah yesh? Sheboth!* '

'I plucked them frae the trees,' said the other weakly, and giggled. 'Fig leaves.' He lurched abruptly forward, the leaves fluttering around him, and the old Jew caught him and lowered him slowly to the earth. His cuts were still filthy, though he was perspiring so much that some of the dirt had simply dripped off with the sweat; Uri snatched up his waterskin and rinsed the rest off, grimacing at the ragged gashes in the other's arms. Working quickly, he took the largest of the fig leaves and pressed them against the cuts, securing them with the pieces of grapevine the other one had brought as makeshift twine. Thank God the sky was clear tonight: the waning moon was still gibbous, and it gave a good light. The whole business took perhaps ten minutes.

'*Az, atah muṭav*, Ciaran,' he said as he finished. '*Hen?* '

The *goy*'s eyelids fluttered, but he didn't say anything. The Jew sat and watched him. His breathing grew quieter; the heavens revolved; the wind changed, shifting to the east and growing a little stronger. Uri bit his lip, wondering whether he should keep watch in case there were something the other one needed, or simply go to sleep. There probably wasn't much he could do to help, no matter what should happen. Unless the wolves should come back … With a sigh, he stood up, stamping his feet to get the feeling back into them (and wincing again at the pain in his ankle), and began walking gingerly around the fire to keep awake.

Perhaps an hour had passed when Uri heard an irregular murmur from Ciaran. He went over and bent down close to him.

'*Atah muṭav?*' he asked; and then, gritting his teeth, he added, '*Chaver?*' Friend?

Ciaran coughed, and said, in a voice that was barely audible over the breeze, 'Did I ever tell thee how I came to be deathless?'

'*Lo.*'

He licked his cracked lips and went on. 'I met the devil one night. He said he'd come to take me, on account o' my wickedness. An' I was a wicked man indeed, ken: a glutton, a lecher, a brawler, an' a thief. Sometimes I'd be shriven, but …' He coughed again and sighed. 'So I says to the devil, *If ye would have me down to hell, I want one last pint before I go.* And he says, *Alright then sinner, a pint shall ye have,* speakin' all mannerly like.'

'*Lamah?*'

'Bless me, I don't know. Anyway … we goes into the pub, an' I has me pint, nice an' slow. One o' them perfect pints, kennest thou? Thick an' rich like good bread. An' he says to me as we need to go down to hell now, an' I says, *I can't leave without payin' for me pint. Pay for it then,* says he; only I hannae silver an' I tells him so. So—' he chuckled; the noise was like grinding gravel— 'he turns himself into a penny, an' I put him in my pocket where there's a crucifix my grandam gave me, an' he cannae change back on account of it. So I legs it out o' the pub.

'Only he can still speak to me, so he bellows as I didn't pay for my pint at all an' I'm a liar an' to let him go. I says to him, *Well, if ye be the Father o' Lies, that makes me your son an' heir now, aye?* An' the devil, he hemmed an' hawed, but at last he had to say *Aye it does.* An' since the devil himself was indisposed, like, thae made yours truly the regent ae hell; so I banished mesel' frae't for all eternity; an' after I let the devil go.'

Uri chuckled weakly. His companion motioned to the waterskin, and he tipped some water into the rasping man's throat. Ciaran hummed with pleasure and licked his lips again, and continued, a little louder. 'So when I came to die, as a man maun, I met me angel an' said, *I cannot go to hell, so I must be heavenbound, yea?* Only he says to me, *Nae, ye were a wicked man, an' nae manner o' wickedness can be before the Lord of 'Osts. So ye'll hae to kip in hell.* An' so I goes down to hell, sore afraid an' mournin', an' come to the gates, an' I calls out to the devil as I cannot go to heaven. An' he comes to the gate, pleased as a cat, an' says as there's a law that I cannot come intae hell to rest for all eternity, on account o' my bein' banished by his own regent. So I've been a-stravaigin' these fourteen hundred years.'

The old Jew looked at him through half-closed eyes. '*Atah hametzeth eth zah.*'

Ciaran laughed. 'Yes, yes I did. But 'tis a damn fine story, nae?'

Uri snorted contemptuously.

'Better,' rasped the *goy*, 'than thine, anyhow.'

'*Dhimamah,*' he replied warningly.

'Simply had to mock, didst thou? Couldn't leave Him be?'

'*L'hashthiq!* '

Ciaran opened his mouth as if to go on, but evidently something stopped him; a strange hesitation was in his face, and he slowly closed his lips. A long silence fell. Nothing was heard but the breeze in the few surviving leaves, and the monotone hum of the ugly beetles. Finally, the *goy* did break the silence after all.

'Art thou sorry?'

Another long pause. '*Lo.*'

He smirked. 'Liar.'

A single drop of clear liquid struck the ground between the old Jew's feet: it lay over the dust like the salt sea. Not a sound escaped his mouth.

SUNSET ON YAMATO

The winter was very early that year. Perhaps the migrant waxwings had brought it south with them.

Iriko looked south, over the many streets and the remaining buildings, towards the sea. Ōsakawan lay at the edge of the withered megalopolis, reflecting a greyish light from the dull sky like a piece of blue slate. Behind her, Hiei-yama and Minako-yama stood in front of Biwako, shouldering heavy cloaks of snow. The five rooves of Tōji's pagoda had, so far, received only a dusting; you could still pick out the individual tiles. But the clouds were swollen like pregnant women, and the gloomy rumbling of thunder over the mountains proclaimed their labor pains. It was only mid-morning, but Iriko sighed and began to descend the narrow, aged stairs of the pagoda. Shini had asked her to stop by some time soon in any case, and it would be better to gather what food she could before the snows came.

She stepped out of the tower onto a thin coverlet of snow, the lacquered *geta* she was wearing interposing a thick line of black between white feet and white ground. It was a little more than six kilometers from the shrine complex to Pontochō, or what was left of it, and Iriko was glad to be raised a little above the hoary earth. A large star-like maple leaf had fallen in the snow by her path, brilliant red in color; she paused to look at it.

As she walked by the scarlet walls and stone-grey eaves of the Kitano Tenman-gū, she slowed her pace. It had been a favorite shrine of hers. Most of the lanterns had been pulled down, in a riot not long before the total collapse, but she noted with approval that they had let alone the golden ornament on the friezes and the underside of the eaves. She paused, thinking, and went inside.

The furnishings of the shrine were disarranged and dusty, though not greatly disturbed. Iriko went to a pile of what could have been mistaken for debris, but was in fact a heap of unused *ema*, the wooden prayer talismans that were offered to the *kami* in supplication. She sorted through them, pausing now and then to hold one up to the light, until she found one that felt right: it depicted the one-legged *torii* from the Sannō Shrine in Nagasaki, which should have been destroyed by the atomic bomb, but of which one pillar had mysteriously survived.

Sitting close to a window with the *ema* and a scavenged brush and bottle of ink, she wrote her prayer: the Emperor's health—the fertility of the fields—victory in wars—prosperity for her family—a husband and children—the favor and blessing of the *kami*—the honor of the Japanese nation. Using a piece of string, she hung the prayer with others that remained, and slipped a few coins into the donation box. The Emperor was dead; her parents and her brother Noritaka were dead; the fields were a wasteland; there was no one left to fight or to marry or to collect the coins. As far as she knew, Endō Iriko was the last person left alive in the archipelago. She murmured aloud to herself:

> '*Natsukusa ya*
> *tsuwamonodomo ga*
> *yume no ato.*'

The signs and banners of the Pontochō *hanamachi* were faded, but recognizable. It had been the first of the city's *geiko* districts (so it had claimed), and they had lingered there the longest. Expertly rendered calligraphy promised the customer the finest tea, the best *sake*, the loveliest *shamisen* playing—executed by the loveliest *shamisen* players, of course—that mortal eyes, ears, and palates had ever enjoyed. One shop, which had endured longer than the others thanks to the owner's fanatical devotion to his craft, still displayed a *kimono* in the window: burgundy silk flowed over the model, dotted with an asymmetrical pattern of white *sakura* flowers like little spurts of foam, and there, on the left sleeve, a plover in flight. It would have been perfect for a *geiko* as her April wardrobe, but the last one had died in February, seven months ago now. Iriko knew, as a matter of theory, that some of them might have survived in other places; but she could never have deliberately countenanced the idea that Kyoto should be deprived of *geiko* while any other city was in possession.

At the northeastern corner of the *hanamachi* stood a crude shack—the Kyū no Shi Myōji, its owner called it, having a naturally morbid sense of humor. It had been built over the wreckage of a failed bar, but with a smaller footprint, so that broken pieces of metal and wood lay about the walls. Iriko stepped lightly over the debris and came to the shack's doorway, which was obscured by a length of midnight blue cloth with *kanji* and *kana* dyed into it:

九 の 四

Iriko suppressed a shiver and called into the shack.

'*Shini-sama, ohayō gozaimasu. Iriko desu.*'

'*Ohairi kudasai,*' murmured a deep voice from the rear of the shack. Iriko lifted her hand and pushed the curtain aside, and stepped in.

Two vases stood at either side of the doorway: one mostly held spidery red *higambana*, the other the palest *kiku* flowers. Each vase was deftly arranged with a single alien blossom in its center: among the *higambana* was a tall white *kānēshon*, and one crimson *tsubaki* emerged from among the *kikubana* like the sun parting a bank of clouds.

The rest of the shack was practically empty, except for a paper lantern suspended from the ceiling. The walls were unadorned, and nothing covered the floor except *tatami* mats. Iriko slipped off her *geta* at the doorway and bowed deeply to the man in the rear of the shack, until the sleeves of her *haori* touched the ground. His *kimono* was white with a black border, and he wore the right breast over the left, as if he were a corpse. He was not looking at her; he was studying the large iron pot that rested in the *ro*, the square opening in the floor that served as a kind of hearth, where he appeared to be boiling water. The small collection of items to his left supported this: they included three hand-made *chawan*, a perfectly cubical black-lacquered *usuchaki*, and a delicate bamboo whisk whose loops were as fine as hairs.

'*O-chadō desu ka, Shini-sama?*' she asked.

The man chuckled. '*Iie, miko-chan. Tan'ni o-cha.*' *Not tea ceremony, my dear shamaness; just tea.* He lifted the cast-iron *tetsubin* from the *ro* and began to prepare the three cups of tea that sat beside him. '*Suwatte kudasai.*'

She knelt and sat back, wondering whom the third cup was for. Shini reached over and opened another wooden box, which contained a few young *koi* fish; he placed these over the *ro* to cook.

'*Phuyu no otozure ga hayaka tsu,*' he remarked.

'*Hai, ue-sama.*'

'*Anata wa sore ga sukidesu ka?*'

'*Chigau, ue-sama,*' Iriko replied. '*Natsu ga koishii.*'

The man smiled, turning the *koi* over with a long pair of chopsticks. '*Mochiron.*' He pushed a steaming bowl of tea towards her. She picked it up, closing her eyes as the heat seeped through the faintly irregular walls of the *chawan* and into her hands. The reedy-sweet aroma floated over her.

'*Ohayō gozaimasu,*' came another male voice, from outside. The man called Shini did not look up, but he answered: '*Ohairi kudasai.*'

The second guest entered. He was a tall, broad-shouldered man, with wild hair and bright eyes. A curious fragrance came with him: a blend of ice, earth, wood, and *kō* smoke. He too wore *kimono*, colored deep green like pine needles, and stood on single-toothed *tengu-geta* that raised him so high above the floor that he had to stoop to pass through the curtain. He slid these off, approached his host, and bowed deeply. '*Shini-sama.*'

'*Wagaya e yōkoso, Ohoyamakui-san,*' replied the other, pushing a *chawan* toward him. The newcomer knelt and sat back into a half-lotus posture. Picking up his tea, he asked, with a nod toward Iriko, '*Nanda kore wa, nadeshiko?* '

Shini said that yes, this was the young woman he had spoken of, and that her name was Endō Iriko.

'*Hajimemashite,*' the new guest said to her, bowing his head slightly.

The *miko* tried to smile, and answered politely, '*Yoroshiku onegai shimasu, Ohoyamakui-san.*' Then Shini handed them each a small plate, bearing one of the steaming hot, slightly burnt *koi*, and a pair of chopsticks. He waved a generous hand at his two guests, who said '*Itadakimasu*' and began to eat. Shini drank his tea, but did not eat; he never did.

For a few minutes, they ate and drank silently. The *koi* were followed by small bowls of rice. As she set her bowl down, the young shamaness said, '*Gochiso sama deshita.*'

'*Jōkyō ka de,*' said the other rudely. Shini merely chuckled.

Iriko spoke again. '*Kono koto ni tsuite wa nandesu ka?*'

Their host explained. Both he and Ohoyamakui were interested in taking Iriko in marriage. It was admittedly a very long time since either had consorted with anyone; but Iriko was a fine young woman and, when there had been other inhabitants left in Kyoto, had been a wise and benignant *miko*. Either one of them would be not only happy but proud to wed her.

A little dazed at the idea, she nodded. '*Watakushi wa kangaeru hitsuyō ga arimasu, arigato.*'

'*Mochiron,*' replied Shini generously. He added that Ohoyamakui would be staying in the remains of the city for a short while—and of course, he himself was always there—so that she need not feel rushed.

Iriko nodded again and said something, she didn't know what, and gulped some more tea. The host and the wild man continued talking, but she was distracted. She herself hardly noticed as, a short time later, she made an automatic yet unexceptionably courteous departure.

A brightly-colored sign in *rōmaji* by the broken doors proclaimed: *Lucky Sunshine Grocery*. Bamboo grew from cracks in the parking lot, and massy ivy was wrapping its long, coral-pink fingers around the walls and feeling its way in through the doors. Iriko's *geta* clunked softly against the snow-dusted tarmac; her *hakama* swished about her; she picked her way cautiously over the broken glass and made her way inside, murmuring a brief prayer to Susano'o to hold the storm back a little longer for her sake.

The lights had gone out about a month ago, but a section of the ceiling had fallen in shortly afterward— thankfully, on top of the long-since-worthless perish- ables—so it was still reasonably easy to navigate the place. Let's see: tinned *nishin*. *Umeboshi*. Tinned bamboo shoots. Pickled *daikon*. Rice. *Pokki*—why not. *Sake*. Bottled water. *Matcha*. That was about as much as she could carry; she took it toward the exit, helped herself to a couple of paper bags (they would do as tinder for the fire later), and made the trek back from Pontochō to Tōji. The flurries had just begun again when the temple complex came in sight.

She removed her *geta* and climbed the many steps up the pagoda, listening to the howling of the wind. Reaching the top floor, she set her groceries down by the entrance and went over to light the brazier she had put in—lugging the great cast-iron thing up the stairs had been miserable, but it was better than traipsing up and down five flights every time she wanted drink or food, and the lower floors all had awful drafts. The great bronze statue of Kanzeon, goddess of mercy, loomed in the gathering dark as the storm intensified. Shivering a little, she fetched a stick of incense, lit it at the brazier, and presented it to the goddess with a prostration.

Iriko set some water to boil, and gathered together some of the rice, *umeboshi*, and *sake*. She added a dash of *sake* to the rice—she would have preferred vinegar, but she had run out—and stirred, tasting a grain occasionally, till she was satisfied with the texture. The finished product, placed in the lacquered box she kept as a dish, formed a perfect *hinomaru bentō*, like the old flag, with the little red plum in the center and the white of the rice around it. She poured the rest of the *sake* into the chipped *chawan* that served as her only drinking vessel, knelt down, and stopped. She tried reaching out to eat, but the strength seemed to be gone from her hands and fingers. Seconds lengthened into minutes, and she could not eat. She could hardly move, staring at the *bentō* as it grew cold.

Thunder and wind beat against the windows, like

wild hands on the head of a drum. It could hardly be much later than noon, but the snowstorm was so thick that it might have been dusk. Leaving her untouched meal in the middle of the floor, Iriko pushed herself to her feet, padded over to her *phuton*, and laid down, sinking quickly into a dreamless sleep.

✳ ✳✳

When Iriko woke, the storm had blustered itself out. She sat up. Judging from the shadows and the light, it was very late in the afternoon, perhaps an hour before sunset. Rising, she crossed to the western side of the pagoda and slid open the *shōji*, walking out onto the wood-railed terrace at the northwestern corner. The sky was still grey, but it was now less the grey of steel and more that of pearl. The fragrance of the snow filled her lungs. The sun was descending behind Atago-yama, visible only as a bright blur behind the cloud veil. She rested her elbows on the railing, putting her chin on her hand, and contemplated the mountain.

'*Kombanwa, miko-san,*' said a voice to her left. Iriko started and spun around.

'*O-Ohoyamakui-sama, ēto, kombanwa,*' she stammered. For it was the green-clad visitor of the morning, whose powerful name she had recognized as easily as that of Shini-sama. His tangled black hair came down to his elbows, and the aromatic smell of *kō* rolled off of him like water from the shell of a tortoise.

The huge man chuckled. '*Sumimasen. Yama-san to yonde kudasai.*' He pushed the *shōji* back open and preceded Iriko inside; she noticed that he took off his large *tengu-geta* there on the balcony.

She offered him some rice and *sake*, but he declined, while urging her to partake if she was hungry. At first she thought he was only being polite, but his insistence eventually convinced her that he really did want her to eat. Her *bentō* had dried out, but she found herself ravenous after waking, and she ate and drank her fill. Yama watched her while she ate—not in the greedy manner of a lecher, but with an almost childlike attentiveness, as if the whole process of eating were intensely interesting to him.

'*O-cha, Yama-san, ne?*' she suggested. He smiled and said that yes, he would like some tea. She set about preparing it. There was silence for a few minutes.

'*Ore to kimi wa haerareru, kekkon shindara,*' he said as she began mixing the *matcha* with the boiling water. *You and I would do well together if we married.*

'*Kami to ningen kekkon wa shimemasu ka? Watakushi wa dō narudarō ka?*' answered the shamaness. *A spirit and a mortal, married? What would become of me?*

'*Shinigami-sama wa kami desu,*' replied Yama-san reasonably. '*Kimi wa kare ga nani o suru ka shitte iru.*' *Lord Shinigami is a spirit too; you know what would happen if you paired up with him.*

Iriko pressed her lips together and swallowed. '*Hai. O-shi.*'

'*Un.*' They drank their tea quietly for a few moments.

'*Soshite*—' She fumbled for words and repeated herself. '*Watakushi wa dō narudarō ka, Yama-san?*'

The *kami* hummed to himself. '*Shinkaku ka. Kimi ga Tenko-gami ni narudarō.*' Apotheosis. *You'd become the Fox Spirit.*

'*Ningende wa arimasen, Yama-san?*'

'*Ningende wa arimasen.*'

There was another pregnant pause. '*Kimi wa kore o sukidesu ka?*' he asked, waving a hand around at the top floor of the temple where she was living. '*Shiawase desu ka, Iriko-san?*' *Do you like it here? Are you happy, Iriko?*

She looked into her *chawan* and swallowed a cry of pain. '*Iie,*' she admitted; '*iie—arimasen—*' A solitary tear, bright as a jewel, dropped into her tea.

The other reached out toward her, then suddenly stayed his hand, as if unsure how intimately he might behave. '*Kimi ga teineidearu hitsuyō wa arimasen,*' he told her in a softer voice. '*Ore ni kansuru kagiri, tatemae wa arimasen.*'

The *chawan* slipped from her fingers and thudded onto the worn *tatami* mat she had placed over the floor; a pool of greyish green blossomed outward from its cracked lip. Iriko put her face into her hands and began crying in earnest, her poised reception of her guest lost. Tears seeped through her closed fingers and collected at the tip of her chin, and her shoulders trembled with the taut, wrenching energy of weeping. She felt a large hand settle on her, rough and cold but moving gently, and she crumbled still further. For a little time she knew nothing except hoarse tears, the firmness of an embracing body, and soft, cooing words of comfort, half-understood.

Eventually the *miko* composed herself and sat up, saying, '*Gomen. Honto ni mōshi wakenai.*'

Ohoyamakui smiled at her. '*Kimi wa shazai suru hitsuyō wa arimasen.*' He stood up, and went out onto the balcony again. Iriko followed him, breathing slowly to maintain her self-mastery.

'*Mu kotaeru,*' he said, sliding his tall *tengu-geta* back on, '*mu kyō.*' *You needn't answer today.* He bowed to her, and she bowed in response. He leapt lightly up onto the wooden railing, landing with perfect balance on the narrow teeth of his *geta*. Then, he leapt again, seeming to twist and elongate as he did so; in only a moment, the towering man had transformed into a gigantic, shimmering sea-green dragon, curling around and soaring through the air away from Tōji in the direction of the rising sun.

'*Seiryū,*' she murmured: *the Azure Dragon,* one of the four protectors of Kyoto. For a long time the shamaness stood and watched him grow smaller in the east, flying toward the temple at Kiyomizu. Finally, as the sky grew bloody with the dusk, she became cold, stirred, and went back in, closing the *shōji* behind her.

✳ ✳✳

The next morning, Iriko awoke with the dawn. She rose, wrapping her *kimono* tightly around her, went over to the pool that lay beneath the statue of Kanzeon, and performed the *temizu* purification, singing quietly as she did so.

'Takama-no-Hara ni kamuzumarimasu
kamurogi kamuromi no mikoto mochite
sume mi oya kamu Izanagi-no-Mikoto
tsukushi no himuka no tachibana no odo no ahagihara ni
misogi harae tamaishi toki aremaseru ...'

It had grown overcast again, but no more snow had fallen. She sat by the brazier as she ate her morning rice and *nishin*, rubbing her feet against one another, thinking.

After she had eaten, Iriko went back down toward Pontochō, stepping gingerly through the snow. Thankfully the drifts were thick enough, and the pavement beneath them level enough, that balancing on the elevated *geta* was not difficult so long as she was not careless. She headed for the Kyū no Shi Myōji; she wanted to talk to Shini again. The choice was burdening her like a great bronze weight.

As she passed along the north side of a ruined Buddhist temple, she heard a growling sort of noise. She looked around; nothing was there. She continued walking, a little more slowly, alert.

The noise recurred. This time Iriko was able to pinpoint it, to a street that ran down toward the Shōsei-en Garden. She looked around and picked up a solid chunk of masonry in each hand, and waited. If it were an animal, it would be easy to repel. If it were something else, it wasn't likely to leave her alone until she had confronted it.

Out of the street there lumbered a large moon bear, the white patch on its chest showing against its dark fur like a pair of swan's wings. Iriko swallowed, and steadied her *geta* against the pavement. She could feel the tiny pits and cracks on the surface of the pieces of stone she was holding, and their edges dug into her palms. She had never been a strong runner. She narrowed her eyes against the light that was reflected off the surrounding snow.

The bear saw her. It made an ugly roaring noise, like a saw being dragged through bone, and began to run at her. She screamed—whether more with rage or terror, she could not tell—and hurled one of the stones forward with all her might. It struck the bear on the side of its head, and the carnivore howled and kept its course. Iriko took the second stone from her left hand, inhaled deeply, and threw.

An indistinct white shape suddenly interposed itself between the *miko* and the bear, and was struck. The hunk of masonry shattered like a firework, and the bear let loose a bark of alarm. The shape was Shini, facing the moon bear; the stone had broken against his white-clad back. He took a slow step towards the animal.

'*Nete kudasai,*' Shini said quietly. The bear obediently laid down and closed its eyes. He approached it and stooped a little, laying a hand on its head above the mangy fringe of fur behind its ears. A brief, sharp gust of wind came out of the west, making Iriko's breath catch as she watched. The bear slumped a little further, into a posture that looked impossibly ungainly, and was still.

Shini straightened up and turned to Iriko. He was not exactly smiling—he never *quite* smiled—but there was a warmth of welcome in his face that almost amounted to a smile. '*Kuma wa mō anata o kinishinaidarō.*'

'*Ēto,*' she gasped; and then, collecting herself, '*arigato gozaimasu, Shini-sama.*'

'*Mochiron.*' He turned and began heading back toward the Kyū no Shi Myōji. The shamaness followed.

✳   ✳✳

'*Sentaku wa anata shidaidesu. Watashi wa kanshō suru koto wa arimasen.*'

'*Wakarimasu, ue-sama,*' replied Iriko. '*Watakushi wa ikutsu ka no adobaisu o onegaishimasu kedo.*'

'*Nan'notameni? Miko-san wa, ryōhō no kettei no kekka o shirimasu.*' *What for? Shamaness, you know the outcome of either decision.*

'*Hai, ue-sama. Demo ...*' She couldn't think how to explain it. A breeze pressed against the western wall of the house, making the *shōji* creak. Shini, seated on the opposite side of the *ro* from her, added a few more coals to the brazier. Then he leaned slightly forward, his hands held as if in the *semui-in* gesture of protection and courage.

'*Iki subarashii,*' he told her; '*watashi wa dare yori mo sore wa yoku shitte imasu. Maikai, zentai no tabi o sanshō shite kudasai.*' *Life is magnificent; I know that better than anyone. I see its whole journey every time.*

Iriko looked at the floor. '*Soshite tsugini nani ga okorimasu ka?*' *And what happens next?*

'*Shiranai.*' *I don't know.*

She stared. '*Ue-sama wa shirimasen ka?*' she said in disbelief. '*Sore muri.*'

'*Hikikaete. Watashi wa Shinigami, shigo o sekai demo Yomi-no-kuni demo nai. Shiranai.*'

'*Sumimasen, demo watakushi wa sore o shinjite imasen,*' Iriko told him icily.

The *kami* said in a gentle voice, '*Sore wa otaku no mondaidesu.*'

The shamaness stood up. No advice, no answers, no future—she almost wished she had been killed by the moon bear. That at least was something decisive. '*Shini-sama wa watakushi no inochi o sukuimashita,*' she said bitterly. '*Kikan no idaina saimu o otte imasu.*'

'*Otaku wa onore ni nani no karite imasen,*' he said placidly: *You owe me nothing.*

Iriko stood quite still for a moment, mastering the pure, liquid anger that was trying to flow from her eyes.

She succeeded. She bowed wordlessly to Shini, padded over the cool *tatami* mats, slipped on her *geta*, and stalked out into the snow under the greying, windswept sky. The cold plucked at her *hakama* like a neglected lover, and she pulled her *haori* closer about her shoulders, setting her jaw and squinting against the gusts of loose snowflakes. Her breath steamed and curled about her, forming the long barbels of a dragon.

As she drew close to Tōji, her steps slowed. Her chaotic emotions of the last hour had not settled; she felt the need to walk further, to expend more energy before she could rest. She stepped into a shop—its locks had rusted so badly that they gave at a firm push—and helped herself to a coat. She walked to the west, into the wind, pretending to take no notice of it.

* **

The Catholic cemetery was small; even a city the size of Kyoto only held so many Christians. And some of them did prefer to be cremated, as Japanese tradition dictated, rather than buried. But her brother Noritaka, who had been baptized with the *tenshi* name *Serafieru*, had been nothing if not doctrinaire and had insisted on a western-style funeral. Many of the headstones were leaning at strange angles, and some were broken, but her brother's granite cross was intact save for one chipped arm. A large *nana-kamado* tree, bright with scarlet berries, towered benignly over the dead.

There was a small bench across from her brother's grave. Iriko sat. She looked at the familiar, slightly worn down *kana* on the headstone, showing his *kaimyō*, the death-name, and his Christian name:

フドオ・ノ・キリヌロ: シサイ・マイケル

Phudō no Kirinuro
Shisai Serafieru

And then, a little lower, in *rōmaji*:

GLORIA DEI EST VIVENS HOMO

'*Kami-sama no eikō ga ikite iru otokodesu,*' she translated. A strange phrase to choose as an epitaph. Glory seemed to have little enough to do with Noritaka's own end: cancerous, vomiting, delirious, flecked with lesions. She could still see the weak hands fumbling over the prayer beads, could hear the slurred and mumbled recitation, mixing Latin in with Japanese and losing track of where he was and starting again. The alkaline smell of hospital cleansers. The whitish, ugly light in the halls. The dull and heavy hours of waiting, worse than active pain, as machines beeped and clicked, neither silence nor music nor speech.

It had all happened before the real disaster began, but Iriko had a curious sense that it had carried her through the disaster. She had watched her brother die and she had not broken; she had not, because he had not. He had sometimes seemed weary, confused often enough, but never afraid. Noritaka had faced death with something more than resignation. It was something like pride, but that wasn't quite it; and it was more active and deliberate than what men usually call *being at peace*. Iriko wondered what he would have advised her.

A waxwing fluttered down from the tree and perched neatly atop her brother's tombstone. She smiled. It was an unusually fine specimen of the species: glossy pearl-grey plumage on the breast rose into black stripes at the throat and the eye, and the head bore rosy touches of orange at the crest. One dark amber eye affixed itself to her with friendly curiosity. It keened sweetly to her.

'*Konnichi-wa*,' Iriko told it.

It cocked its head, then fluttered back up into the gravid branches of the *nana-kamado*. Iriko gazed into the west, where the sun was glowing faintly through the clouds.

The waxwing chirped again, and she turned. It was on the ground between her and Noritaka's tombstone, clutching a little sprig of berries in its beak. The bird hopped closer to her, and then right up onto the bench.

'*Hai, tori-san?*'

It dropped the berries into her lap, chirped once more, and flew away. Iriko's eyes followed it for a few moments, and then fell to the clutch of fruit it had left behind. Nestled among the berries was a single, withering blossom—apparently the bees had missed it. She couldn't think why it had not fallen off with the rest in the earlier autumn; perhaps it had been held back by the berries that surrounded it. Its petals, wilted though they were, still showed creamy white against the brave red of their neighbors. Iriko plucked one of the berries and tasted it, tart and sweet and cold. She plucked another.

The wind breathed over her, and the last dying blossom was dislodged. It soared and spun, and was gone. She almost moved to catch it, but something made her stop.

'*Chiru*,' she quoted quietly, '*koso hana to*.' *Falling is the essence of a flower*. Of course.

Iriko rose and walked back to the *hanamachi*.

✳ ✳✳

As the shamaness approached the Kyū no Shi Myōji, the shimmering figure of the dragon stood out vividly against the pale sky. She saw him at the periphery of her vision, but her eyes stayed level, fixed on the gently moving curtain of the distant hut.

When Iriko reached it, she slipped off her *geta* and pushed aside the curtain. The hut was different now: the lantern had been extinguished, and the *tatami* mats had been moved to conceal the *ro*. It was cold. Shini sat at the rear of the hut, a vast pale shape with head bowed, one hand in his lap and the other touching the floor beside him. Dimly, she could distinguish three small drinking bowls of unequal size before him—*sakazuki*—and a flask of *sake*. He had foreseen her decision.

'*Kombanwa, Shinigami-sama.*'

'*Kombanwa, Endō-san.*'

He lifted the flask and handed it to her. She poured *sake* into the smallest of the *sakazuki*, and he lifted it in both hands and said, '*Izanagi-sama to Izanami-sama, shōnin desu.*' Then he sipped from it one, two, three times, and passed the vessel to Iriko.

She took it, with a slight, courteous bow of her head, and declaimed, '*Izanagi-no-Okami to Izanami-no-Mikoto, uchira ni minashite kudasai.*' She drank.

Shini filled the second *sakazuki*, and this time she invoked the *kami* and sipped the liquor first, and he responded. Then she filled the last and largest vessel, and again he prayed and drank, and again she did likewise.

As the marriage rite concluded, through the immense silence of the winter, the fragrance of *kō* wafted into the hut from outside. It was Ohoyamakui, saying goodbye. The faintest hint of the sunset touched the darkened room through the door behind the shamaness, dyeing the chamber a reddish gold.

Iriko set the *sakazuki* down and looked at her husband. '*Kaimyō wa watakushi ga motte imasu ka?*' Am I to *have a death-name?*

Shinigami reached into his *kimono* and pulled out a piece of paper with a pair of elegantly penned *kanji* on it:

人類
Man

Outside, the air became still. A waxwing suddenly darted up from the roof of the hut and vanished into the darkening sky.

THE MOTHER AND THE WENDIGO

Wapayâw laid her palm on her stomach with a wince. She was still hungry.

Around her stretched the vast *iyû ashîy*: a flat, colossal, impossible space of grass and shrubs and expired flowers, all golden-grey in the autumn sun, running out as far as the eye could see, save for the foothills of the clay-layered badlands away to her right. It was early. Wapayâw looked behind her, back into the north, where spruces and ancient pines gazed sternly south, watchmen against the heat and the weird beasts of the *maskotew*; the edge of the forest could still be picked out against a bulwark of hills. She sighed, nodded a kind of farewell to the trees, and turned around again.

Her people, the people of Wawastew township, had cast her out—the horrible names they called her still screamed in her ears: glutton, thief. Wapayâw had tried to calm them; but in the end, they refused to give her any more food and compelled her to leave their village.

She cringed a little at the thought of going to the *wamishtikôshiw* for food. Not that they were cruel or arrogant—well, not these days, anyway. But they did tend to be so elaborately civil, in their own way, as if they were trying to make up for something it was bad form to speak frankly about. She thought sourly that she knew very well what that was, and would have preferred them to be openly apologetic. Or better, openly unapologetic, since they felt guilty but weren't penitent. The only real penance (as Wapayâw saw things) would be to pack up and go back to where they came from all those centuries ago. But they would never do anything so costly. Costs were for other peoples to bear.

She suddenly recollected herself; she had been walking without even seeing where she was going. A nasty little blue-black mosquito had settled on her arm, and she swatted it with grim pleasure. The dried-out grasses were thick, too limp and yet too massed for her switch to clear a path effectively. She trudged onward, looking for a road.

A slight movement in the expanse of drab grasses. Something white and small. Wapayâw paused, watching patiently. It was a young hare, apparently still making its way back to its nest for the day. The woman held herself quite still. It came to within a few yards of her, and suddenly sat back on its haunches, its sandy-colored ears twitching. The hare's black, liquid eyes thrummed with vigilance as it looked at her—or seemed to look, for the creature showed no reaction to the woman's presence. She struck quickly.

The hare didn't get much chance to struggle; Wapayâw's fingers were deft and powerful. She had never much cared for uncooked meat, but she had no flint, and anyway she couldn't have carried fuel with her for more than a few days. Ripping through the skin with her nails, she tore the flesh from the hare's bones eagerly with her teeth, searching out every morsel her tongue could find. When the meat was gone, she cracked open the larger bones and sucked out the marrow, and licked the bones and her lips and fingers afterward. It wasn't really enough, but it helped.

A long gap in the grasses revealed the presence of a road. It would take the better part of an hour to reach it, but it would be far easier to travel on than the deceptively yielding earth of the prairie, so long as it was not too ruinous to serve its purpose.

Once Wapayâw reached it, the road turned out to be usable if long neglected. The asphalt was crazed and faded, and dead weeds straggled through the cracks. She accidentally kicked a stray piece of concrete as she walked, and it was so frangible that it broke as soon as it hit another piece of rock.

The hours wore on. She trudged south. The sun

inched his way up into the middle of the sky, coaxing a little warmth into the numb mass of air that had sunk from the region of the Kisiskâciwani-Sîpiy toward the plains; then, inexorably, he began to slip toward the mountains and the horizon.

Wapayâw thought of her daughter and son, Matisa and Kika, who had been taken from her—kept behind in Wawastew with their grandfather, a medicine man. Her husband, a man called Misiwâpos, had contracted the *moncosak* disease not long after his son was conceived: he had lived to see Kika's birth, and name him, and then died. It had been less than a year afterward that the village began to turn against her; she suspected that her sister-in-law, who had always been jealous of her, had begun telling tales. It was certainly she who first accused Wapayâw of orchestrating Misiwâpos' death by witchcraft.

Matisa was only six, but already one could see that she would grow into a great beauty. Her hair was as brilliant as black silk, and her shapely young body was at once plump and strong, as a girl's should be, preparing for the day when she too would nurture life from her body. And she was such a lively, light-hearted child, the sort who always had feathers and flowers in her braids. Kika, as beautiful as his sister, was her opposite—quiet even as a baby, his eyes always heavy with thought, with cunning little limbs and probing fingers. The foresight of mothers told Wapayâw that he would go into the city and become a scholar.

The woman had begged to take her children with her. They had already lost their father: must their mother too be taken away? But Matisa and Kika had remained in the arms of their grandfather as she tore a farewell from her throat, taking with her just two small keepsakes to remind her of them, dangling from her belt like amulets.

A week ago, the reverie would have made her cry, but the monotony of grief had grown too much for that. Now she simply remembered it all. It was almost ritual. The memories had a peculiar clarity of perception: the colors, the textures, the scents, the music of each voice, were all vivid to her mind, as if they were strange to her and yet not strange. Grief could do that; she knew that well from Misiwâpos' death.

Suddenly she saw that, far ahead, there was a truck on the road. It was not traveling. Perhaps it had stalled, or the owner was answering nature's call. Wapayâw quickened her pace a little; she needed food, and more than that, she felt the need of company.

As she drew closer, she could see that the truck was quite an old one, and not well maintained. The paint was peeling freely, the tires were sagging, and there were large patches of rust on the fenders and the edges of the bed. Perhaps it was only a wreck—no, there was the top of the driver's head. At least, there was his hat, one of those brightly-colored plastic hemispheres that men wore when they tore buildings apart. Her enthusiasm for requesting a ride had evaporated, but she decided to ask for the lay of the land in any case. And whether he had any food to spare.

Wapayâw came up to the door and knocked on it sharply. 'Hello there!' she said in English. 'Can you tell me where I am?'

The man in the car sat utterly still; his eyes were open, but he didn't so much as blink when she banged and shouted. She struck the window till the glass shattered and then broke, and at last, his head moved: a brief, sickening lurch to the left and down, dislodging a small cloud of flies.

Though she was shocked for a moment, Wapayâw was not horrified. She had seen death many times, and the Christians and the medicine men she had known in her village would both have given her—yes, incompatible, yes, dissimilar, yet—beautiful and dignified ways of greeting death and the dead. *Ayiwepiwin, ahcâhk, ayiwepiwin,* she thought to herself, remembering the leaden, throaty drone of the old women, intoned while the medicine men performed the Wendigo Dance. The stricter Christians among them said the dance should not be performed at all, but no one took any notice of that. Better to multiply divine aids than divide them, everyone else felt. And indeed, their clutch of tutelary spirits included Nanabush, Mannie the Virgin, Chamindo, Manito, and the Healing Angel, for whom Wapayâw's parents had named her.

She shook herself again. Reverie was becoming addictive. It was the solitude that did it. She looked at the corpse. It was sad to think of him here, alone in his last few hours. Curiously, the body did not smell bad; perhaps the dryness had partially mummified it? She would have buried him, but she had no shovel. She bowed her head and intoned a spell her father had taught her, to ease and prosper the journey of the dead into the invisible world: '*Meita sowus ote peyepo tepâte, tuta mâsiyo koto, weci pîse: motewo koto, powey powase.*' As far as she knew the words were gibberish, but if it could help she would put it at his disposal.

✶　✶✶

Wapayâw resumed her trek south, munching on *pimîhkân* she had found in the truck. She had seen no other people or animals since the morning. She cast a glance toward the sunset, its colors muted by the inky clouds that so often covered the sky like pockmarks of late. Her shadow, thrown fantastically out toward the eastern horizon, plodded with her. She sighed, hoping that there would be a village or a town soon, and that she might sleep in a bed again for a change.

No: not *her* shadow. She stopped and looked.

It was gigantic, vaguely primate in shape, but with claws and tangling antlers; its belly was grotesquely bloated, while the thing's limbs were skeletal. Wapayâw looked to her right, but there was nothing there. She looked back at the vast black form; the sheer size of the thing made her want to shudder. It wasn't just the elongation of dusk—she knew that too well to be misled. This was the shape of a monster, like the *skookum* of the legends of the Chinook out west, or the emaciated *wendigo* that could prey on warriors as if they were children, seizing them with its steel-strong fingers and ripping them open to devour their viscera. Her fingers brushed against the images of Matisa and Kika at her waist, and she whispered a protective invocation to Chamindo. The *wendigo* might be invisible, but it was not invulnerable.

A faint noise as of many whispering voices met Wapayâw's ears. She ignored it firmly and continued her march southwards. A tooth suddenly struck her finger, and she gave a sharp, short cry, looking down at her hands—but she had merely finished the *pimîhkân* sooner than she had expected and accidentally bitten her finger as she did so.

* * *

Two days later there was a village. A little after dawn, under a thin layer of white clouds, Wapayâw came upon a weatherbeaten sign that read *W come to Coffe reek!*, standing at the northern edge of the settlement; the place could hardly have more than three dozen buildings in it. She looked around the handful of streets, houses, and shops, calling out to discover any survivors. No one answered.

She decided to try the doors. Few were locked, and

none were sturdy enough to keep her out in any event. The houses were all empty of people; one did have a pair of dogs in it, which the owners had apparently poisoned as a form of euthanasia, but that was all. There weren't many other buildings: a general store. A tiny gas station. A clinic whose automatic doors were broken, with a large brown rat sniffing around the entryway. The rat looked up at her, squeaked shrilly, and scampered away.

She went to the defunct general store and picked at the remaining supplies it contained. She had expected an insufferable smell, but it seemed clean enough despite the long neglect that had decayed its doors and windows. There was a good deal of tinned meat and fish, some vegetables that had once been frozen, some *mahtâmin*, a little honey (though she had to pick her way around a jar that had fallen to the floor and shattered). She had been hoping that, if Coffee Creek had any survivors, they would have camped out there—no such luck.

As Wapayâw was leaving, she saw the shape again, incompletely reflected in a broken window. Greyish skin pulled taut over inhumanly large bones, insectile fingers wandering near its belly. She turned around, but there was nothing. Slowly, warily, she turned back to the broken window. The *wendigo* seemed to be watching her, though she could not see its face. Coming closer. She reached out toward the broken glass.

There was a sharp cry. It was a child's voice. Wapayâw spun around. There was no sign of the *wendigo*; a grubby young *wamistukusuw* girl was scrambling out from under a tilted box of onions, her eyes fixed on the door.

'*Mo cêskwa!*' the woman called without thinking, and then switched to English. 'Wait a minute!'

The girl flew. Wapayâw ran after her, hoping she could reach the child before the monster did. The door swung open, and the fresh sunlight struck her like a blow; the clouds had melted, and the air was dazzling now. She paused, blinking. She looked back into the general store, but could only see a vague dimness behind popping circles of orange—afterimages. She waited a few seconds for her eyes to adjust. Slowly, her focus returned, just in time to see the girl dart around the corner of a distant house.

Wapayâw ran forward. The pattering footsteps ahead told her the *wamistukusuw* was still running; she too must have seen whatever it was. The woman grasped her little figurine of Matisa and recited a charm to protect both herself and the little girl.

A tell-tale bang and rattling noise announced that a light metal door had been opened and allowed to swing shut again. Perhaps one of the houses was occupied after all. Wapayâw listened, searched, even sniffed, among the roads and the worn lawns of the hamlet. After minutes of cautiously silent tracking, her ears caught a sobbing voice, babbling in between gasps about a monster. There was a shutter hanging askew from an attic window, and the voice was coming from there; and sure enough, as

Wapayâw approached, she noticed a stained storm-door over a concrete stoop. She crept up along the side of the house and listened.

'… huge and grey all over and with these big things like antlers,' she was saying, 'and it had little dried-up *heads* hanging on it! There was blood all over its chin and its face, and all on its fingers, with these awful claws. It tried to grab me, it was going to eat me! It wants to eat me!'

'Okay,' a man's voice answered, 'it's okay, calm down, honey. You're safe now, it's okay.' The sound of the girl's crying became muffled, and the male voice crooned softly. Wapayâw could not help but tear up a little—there was a peculiar sweetness to her in hearing a father comforting his daughter. It made her think of Misiwâpos and how he had been with Matisa, before he became sick. The father hummed and cooed and worked his little girl down from her terror.

There was a loud clacking noise that, at first, Wapayâw could not place, although she knew she recognized it. The man spoke. 'I'm going out to find it. You stay here and stay as quiet as you can, okay? I'll be back once the monster is dead. I won't let it hurt you. Hey. Be brave for me, okay honey?'

'Okay.' Still shaken, but being brave.

'I'll be right back.' There was a clomping sound of boots on stairs.

Wapayâw decided to meet him at the door, to help him look. She had never quite spotted the creature, but two hunters were always better than one. Better not to stand right in front of the door, though—it might startle him, and he had a gun. Oh, of course: that was what the clacking had been, a shotgun being pumped. She couldn't think why she had not recognized the sound at once. She stood upright and stepped forward from the side of the house, toward the storm-door.

The man pushed the door open; he wore a deerskin jacket and a white shirt. For a moment, in the glass of the upper window-pane, Wapayâw spotted her reflection.

She saw the huge grey belly, the inhuman antlers, and the spidering fingers of the *wendigo* that had loomed in the broken glass of the supermarket. She saw her own emaciated hands pulling apart the organs and muscles of the dead man in the truck, ripping him into strips like so much *pimîhkân*. She saw her father's eviscerated body, and the headless corpses of Kika and Matisa on his arms; she saw Misiwâpos' sister advancing on her amid the reek of burning sage, her face set and pale, decked in the feathers of the medicine woman and brandishing a worn statuette of Mannie and Chamindo. There were torches and screaming.

Wapayâw stumbled and recollected herself. Hallucinations! She must be going mad. A white-tailed buck had come out of the house through the door; something about it bothered her, she couldn't remember what. It turned to face her with a scream. She charged the beast, but it stood its ground, and suddenly she and the deer were wrestling on the earth, but there were too many hands, and its antler must have punctured her at some point because there was a terrible pain in her shoulder and bleeding hands on a throat that screamed like a human the way deer do the way they screamed in Wawastew ripped out of throats torn from

SEAFARERS

'There's no way, Mike. No way in hell.'

The sun was shining, and there was a fine breeze coming from the south. Pleasant days were always becoming fewer and further between; but the light glistened on the bay like it had in the old days. The double-faced wooden idol, which had provoked their conversation by washing up on the beach, sat between them: one face had a pinecone-like headdress above and something like an octopus or a squid below, while the other was surmounted by an intricately inscribed circle and had inward-pointing triangular panels around its eyes. Its gaping mouths were crusted with the salt residue of seawater. Mike had recognized it as a depiction of two Oceanian gods, and this (to Tom's bewilderment) had somehow led to a discussion of sailing halfway across the Pacific in a raft of their own making.

'It's been done,' Mike insisted to Tom. 'Not that it's easy, of course—'

'*Claro que sí*, as long as we admit it's not easy, it secretly will be.'

'Exactly. Look, the Polynesians used to do this kind of thing all the time, it's how they spread all over. And back in the Modern period people would do the same thing, to set a record or whatever.' He picked up the statue and rubbed it with his thumbs, almost caressing it. 'If we build it right, and prep carefully, we could make it in just a hair under a month. I'm sure of it.'

'And what makes you so certain Hawaii is safe, anyway?'

'The currents in that part of the ocean. I took some oceanography classes while I was studying for my master's, and there's this thing, it's called the, the—the North Pacific Gyre, that's it.' He pulled his fingers through the coarse sand, one wobbling curve representing the Californian coast and a series of dots representing Hawaii; Mike followed this with a rapid circling motion of his hand that apparently stood for the movement of the Gyre, well removed from the islands. 'Anyway, it's like this whirlpool sort of pattern of currents, and the point is, it should probably have directed all the worst of the fallout and stuff way to the south of Hawaii. Worst case scenario, the east edge of the big island got hit and lost some plant life, and the animals probably migrated westwards.'

Tomás fingered the little gold cross he always wore

around his neck. He did not look satisfied. Mike pressed on. 'Well, what do you want to do, then? Stay here? Don't get me wrong, *hermano,*' he said, incorrectly enunciating the *h*—

'You know I hate it when you call me that—'

'—I do like Monterey, but we're starting to see things going wrong here, too. You know, the fish, the seals? The seaweed? We can't stay here much longer.'

Tom smiled bitterly. He had started to think, naïvely maybe, that they could do just that. The slow trek north from Los Angeles after his husband's death had been chaotic and occasionally violent, until they had passed Big Sur; after that, the peacefulness of the suddenly empty California coast had been like magic. 'Dying at sea is an extremely nasty way to go, *chico.* Between thirst, exposure, and exhaustion, you'll start hoping for the sharks. Personally I'd rather die on land in relative comfort.'

'I really wish you wouldn't make jokes like that,' Mike told him, pulling a face. Tomás blushed slightly, and gestured to his friend to go on. 'There's no reason for us to die at all.'

'How long would it take to build a raft?'

'With the materials we've got here, a week, I guess? If we work hard. There's not much else to do, so I'm optimistic.'

'You are a perpetual optimist.'

'I'm always amazed,' Mike said with relish, 'at the

way you make "optimist" sound like "*pendejo.*" It's like a crabby superpower.'

'*Ay, cállate.*'

'Look. Say two or three days to gather enough wood and rope and flotation stuff, and scrounge up some cloth to make a sail with. We can use a lot of pieces from the wrecked boats at the Wharf, I bet. Then a few days of construction. A day or two of test sailing, like down to Carmel and back, maybe, see how the craft handles. Then another few days to gather supplies. We'll need water and a good deal of dried food, and stuff to fish with.'

'Speaking of water, how are we supposed to get that while we're sailing? It hardly seems like we could take enough with us for, what was it, a month? That's like thirty gallons we'll need.'

'More, actually, since we'll be out in the weather all the time. Say forty gallons for the both of us. And we should probably plan on losing some too. But,' he went on, waving down a tired, disbelieving laugh from Tom, 'sometimes we'll be able to collect rainwater, so we do that when we can and make that our first source; and whenever we manage to catch fish, there's a watery fluid in their eyes and spines that you can straight-up drink. Only when neither of those is enough do we dip into our stash, see? And if we fish we can cut down a little on our food store, too. Mostly dried fruit—it's light, and there's no point getting scurvy on our way to sexy Hawaiian beaches.'

Tom rolled his eyes, and made a gesture that people usually reserve for their enemies, but he smiled all the same.

'Come on, *hermano*. What d'you say?'

He paused, fidgeting with his cross again, and then said slowly, 'If there are any of those big plastic oil drums left in the cannery, and something to caulk them with, they'd be ideal as flotation devices. We'll need at least four—'

Mike leapt to his feet, punching the air and whooping. Tom smiled again, and studied the idol, its worn surfaces feeling almost soft.

*   **

A few hours later, Tom was sitting on one of the great ragged rocks that dotted the bay, looking west. The surf broke gently beneath his feet. The sun was sinking into the ocean, dyeing it the color of a blood orange, and the sky all around radiated with shades of rose and gold and greyish violet, fading to a deep Persian blue at the periphery of his vision. To his left, where the coast curved outwards toward Point Pinos, the rocks and cypresses looked like surrealist paintings, their seaward faces burnt yellow and their eastern ones dead black.

There was a scrabbling noise, and Mike had heaved himself up onto the rock beside him. 'Hey, everything good?'

'*Sí, sí.* Just watching the sunset is all, nothing crazy.'

'Oh. Okay, yeah. Is it alright if I join you?'

'You don't have to, but,' said Tom, 'yes it's alright.'

Mike nodded. They sat quietly for a few minutes while the magnificent horizon slowly darkened.

Tomás spoke. 'Mind if I ask you something?'

'Sure, go ahead.'

He looked at his fingers. 'Did you ever think about —*aver*, you know …'

'Killing myself?'

He didn't answer. Mike paused, as if he were checking whether he'd ever thought about suicide, and then said, 'Kind of. When Marina was dying, I begged the universe to take me instead. It said no, obviously. But —it's funny, since it was over, I feel like I haven't needed to grieve. Like I did all my grieving while she was in chemo. Don't get me wrong, I miss her pretty bad; but at the same time, I knew her and I got to be with her, and I know it's sappy or whatever but she made everything beautiful. I can't—*waste* that.'

Tom frowned. 'I'm not sure praying to die in place of someone you love is really the same thing.'

'Maybe not. I wouldn't know, I guess. Anyway she was your sister, you knew her a lot longer than I did.' A few gulls screamed off in the distance. 'Do you want to talk about her? Or Brendan?'

Tomás shook his head. '*No gracias.*'

Mike counted in his head, waiting for the words to start pouring out. Exactly as he reached his silent mental *ten*, Tom began to speak again.

'Brendan grew up with his aunt and uncle. He never knew much of anything about his parents, except that his mother named him after a monk from Ireland. She left him this cross; he gave it to me on our second anniversary. Did I ever tell you how we met?'

'No.'

'It was in Paradise. Not like that!' he said, answering Mike's mimed retching. 'The *town* of Paradise, you know, near Chico? Anyway, I was living there at the time with Marina, doing my nursing internship. One day this guy gets brought into the ER; he's very good-looking, but he's taken a nasty spill during a hike and has lacerations all down his left side from rocks and gravel he'd fallen on. So I put some painkillers in him and go to dress the cuts, and as I'm putting a bandage on his thigh he grabs my hand and says, "Careful, handsome," and then passes out from the meds and shock.'

'And you woke him up with a kiss and got married the next day.'

'Who's telling the story, *¿cabrón?*'

'Okay, I'll be good.'

'So this guy is in the hospital for about a day, and he's really flirty with me the whole time. Well, whenever he's conscious, anyway. I'm glowing but trying to be professional. He gets discharged, I show him out, and he gives me his number. We set up a date for about a week out, because my schedule's so jam-packed. I get to the restaurant we agreed on early because I'm so afraid of being late, it's this tiny Vietnamese place I hadn't tried yet. And if I do say so I was looking *muy guapo*.'

Mike made a whirling *go on* gesture with his hands. Tom sighed and said, 'The bastard stood me up. I waited for over an hour, and between the disappointment and the stress of my internship and everything, I started crying right there in the restaurant. The waiter felt terrible for me—I hadn't actually bought anything, at first because I was waiting and then because I was starting to think I'd, well, been stood up, and the waiter rushes me outside where it's quiet and dark and he gives me a cigarette. So I tell him what happened and calm down a little, and he talks to me about some terrible dates he's had and even gets me laughing a little. So he gives me a hug and—'

'—and then you finally exchange numbers?'

'No, I left, and then *mañana* he calls from the restaurant because I'd left my wallet there. After *that* we exchanged numbers.'

Mike gave a hoot of laughter. 'The original Romeo and Julian setup, huh.'

Tomás smiled. 'It was kind of a whirlwind after that. We had only been dating for five months when Brendan proposed. He said—he said he already knew what he wanted, so why wait?' He sighed. 'Fourteen years. He taught me everything I know about astronomy, he was working on a doctorate in astrophysics, you know.'

'Then why was he working as a waiter? Don't they— I mean, didn't they used to pay you to get advanced degrees? Under the, what was it, the Butler-Scott Plan or whatever?'

'Not every field got those subsidies. Anyway we met way before he went back to school. He was waiting tables to supplement his income as a tutor.' Tom sighed softly. 'Those stupid rioters. We should never have moved back to L.A.'

'But if you hadn't, I'd never have met Marina.'

'Watch it,' Tom said through his teeth.

'Oh, Christ,' Mike said, turning red, 'I'm sorry, I didn't mean it like that.'

'I know you didn't, it's just—look, let's change the subject. Wanna go check the traps?'

'Uh, sure, yeah.'

The two men got up and climbed down the rock back onto the beach, and walked north, along the line of the snares they had set to catch animals for food. Sure enough, the second snare they came to had a seagull trapped in it.

'Are you sure it wouldn't be better to skip dinner tonight?' said Mike.

'We've eaten worse.'

'Have we, though?' Mike replied. He found a rock anyway, and was quick about it.

✶　✶✶

The tide was receding, so they built their fire on the beach that night. There was still plenty of fuel, since they hadn't come anywhere near exhausting the planks from the Fishermen's Wharf. Tom cupped his hands and cautiously lit a match between them (matches being something they could less afford to be careless with), and set it to the kindling. Within a few minutes, a bright little teepee of warmth sat between them, and Mike had finished plucking the gull and started separating the meat from the bones and entrails. The idol, its pinecone-and-octopus side facing them, sat at the edge of the firelight.

'Where are the skewering sticks?'

'In the cabin, I think,' said Tom. "The cabin" was their slightly ridiculous name for the luxurious (and largely intact) Perry House, which they had adopted as their base of operations. 'I'll get them.'

He brought the skewers down the hillside. The cool, salt air rustled the eucalyptus leaves behind him as he returned to the fire. The seagull meat was cold and slippery and stank arrestingly of fish, and getting it onto the skewers was a chore. Once they had done so, they quickly put it into the heart of the fire, to get the smell slightly further from their noses.

'All the perfumes of Arabia cannot clean this little bird.'

Tom smiled. 'Would you ever have tried seagull before this?'

'Sure,' Mike said, 'I mean, I'll try anything once. Why not?'

'*Jesucristo*, where do I begin.'

'Ah, don't be such a bouge. Trying new stuff is how you stay young.'

'I never wanted to be young. I was born a cranky old *ermitaño*. I used to lie awake at night, thinking of fresh ways to grumble at youths.'

Mike laughed, and pulled his skewered rag of meat from the fire. He eyed it, and took an inquisitive bite. 'It's done. And terrible.'

They set to. The sun had fully set, and the last hints of red were sinking after it. The night sky was clear for a change, and took a peppering of stars as they divided the gull, piece by piece. It had been a hungry week.

Once the revolting bird was eaten, Mike told his companion that he had a surprise: he produced a curiously shaped bottle that he had found in one of the deserted houses and had been saving for whatever he could plausibly define as a special occasion. On the bottle were the words *Clase Azul*.

'Finest tequila in North America, even before everything went to shit,' he said.

'*Pinche*,' breathed Tom.

'Not the word I'd have used, but whatever.'

Tom grinned and hit his friend, who hit back. They opened what was literally the best tequila on earth, and passed the bottle back and forth, talking sometimes and sometimes quiet.

Tom reached over for the idol that had prompted their new plans. The sculpture was made from a palm stump (and therefore, Mike had assured him, made relatively recently, since an unprotected palm-wood sculpture would deteriorate quickly in seawater), representing two figures on its opposite faces. Tom asked him to say more about the statuette.

'Well, let me think. This face with the pineapple-looking headdress is Kanaloa, the god of the sea. Sometimes he straight up is the sea, or it's his body in some way. Usually he's the god of the underworld as well, gathers souls. The octopus under him is his animal. And usually he's paired with Kanē, the creator.' He turned the idol around. 'See these triangular eye panels, and the disc in his crown? Those are for the sun. He's the supreme god. Kanē and Kanaloa were important to canoes, too, you prayed to Kanē while you built a canoe and to Kanaloa when you sailed it. You find that a lot in Polynesian mythology, pairs of gods that govern opposite or twinned aspects of things, like death and life, darkness and light, south and north.'

'South and north?'

'Yeah. Including the lines of the tropics, Capricorn and Cancer, you know. You gotta remember, these were seafarers, the points of the compass and being able to read the stars are a big deal.'

'Hm. *Claro*. Go on.'

'That's kind of the gist of Kanaloa, at least the gist of what I studied. Oh, and he teaches magic or something, and sometimes he's the person that mankind got fire from.'

'The god of the *ocean* gave man fire.'

'In some versions. It depends.' He took a swig of tequila and passed the bottle to Tom.

'And Kanē?'

Mike scratched his shoulder. 'Well, I learned less about him, but I know he was the special deity of day and dawn. Made all the other gods, made mankind and breathed life into them. Also his worship was much simpler than that of most other gods, it didn't require sacrifices and rituals.'

'That sounds nice.' Tom set the idol down between them, rotated to show Kanē's more geometric face. 'How many gods are in the Polynesian pantheon, anyway?'

'Hard to say. There were lots of Polynesian pantheons, for one thing—I know the Hawaiian best, and a little bit of Samoan—and the differences between gods and spirits and humans and demigods ... it gets messy. It's a little like the Japanese *kami* that way.'

'Do you have a favorite?'

'You are drunk,' Mike laughed. 'I've never heard you take an interest in this stuff before.'

'*Tengo el derecho a tomar*,' Tom answered, lying down on the coarse sand. An arm passed over him and scooped up the bottle of tequila. He challenged the arm without sitting up, stabbing the air with a menacing finger at each word. '*Derecho. A. Tomar.*'

'Whatever you say, *Señoro Borracho*.'

'*Dios mio*, why do you mess up your Spanish on purpose.' Tom sat up. '*Dámela. La Clase Azuuuuul.*'

Mike grinned and shook his head, but proffered the

bottle anyway. A happy murmur of '*Aaaaazuuul*' was rapidly dunked in liquor. After a long draught, Tom put the bottle down again; he was looking up at the dark blue sky.

'Hey, a meteor,' said Michael.

'It's the Perseids,' Tom said. 'They peak tonight.'

'The Perseids,' said Mike.

'*Sí sí*, they come from the general direction of Perseus, the constellation. Hence, Perseids. Useful way to judge directions and times if you know the stars.'

'Can't you just get what you need from the North Star?'

'Depends on your latitude. If you ever cross the equator then the North Star's invisible. Blocked by the earth's bulge.'

'Dirty.'

Tomás crumpled with laughter.

*　＊＊

The next few days consisted mostly in picking over the least-ruined boats at the Wharf for usable parts. (There was one apparently virtually intact yacht tethered there, but, even aside from uncertainty about fueling the thing and their total inexperience with yachts, Mike and Tom left it alone for the same reason everyone else had: the local sea birds had with one consent adopted it as a toilet.) Boards, nails, caulking, oil drums, ropes, sails, lengths of nylon cord to supply purposes for which rope was too thick. Before the end of the second day, they both had blisters on their hands. 'Like real seamen,' Mike had said, and looked expectantly at Tom, who pointedly ignored it.

Nevertheless, it was Mike who did direct most of the construction of the raft. His advanced degree in Polynesian Studies was still fresh in his brain, and while the materials of ancient rafts had been different, he was able to adapt competently enough for the purpose. Slowly, the raft took shape, and the harsh touch of sun and sand and rope and wood on their hands became both gentler and more austere—calluses took the place of blisters. It was barely a week before the raft construction proper was finished. They named it the *Star of the Sea*, after a church that Brendan had liked. They painted the title a little clumsily on the sail.

The two of them made their trial voyage down to Carmel. When everything went smoothly (itself an unanticipated stroke of good fortune), they made another test trip, this time northward, as far as Swanton. Both of them turned out, against all odds, to be reasonably good natural sailors, and the weather had stayed fair for the most part.

After that it was all gathering supplies and preparing. Compact foods with a lot of proteins, fats, and vitamins were the ideal. Nuts, seeds, pemmican (as much as they hadn't scavenged and eaten already), and dried fruit topped the list, along with lots of water. Less than a week after the raft itself was finished, Mike proposed that they make their decisive assay upon the Pacific Ocean itself, striking out for Hawaii.

'*¿Ay, ahora?*' asked Tom.

'There really isn't much good waiting any longer,' Mike replied. 'I know the seasons don't affect us as much in this climate, but still, with autumn coming on, the open sea won't be as friendly. And anyway, we're getting a little low on supplies here in Monterey. If we do want to stay here over the winter, we'll have to start going further and further out into the countryside to get what we need.' He looked suspiciously at the whitish sky, and popped the last piece of a recently-scavenged Slim Jim into his mouth. 'Capeesh?'

Tom looked around. The sandy hills, the weirdly bent trees, the straggling patches of ice plant, the sea-torn rocks, and, in the furthest distance, the blue-grey peaks of the Sierra Nevada all seemed to lean slightly inwards, as if to hear his reply. '*Claro, sí.*'

'Hey, who knows, *hermano*. Maybe we'll come back some day.'

'*Sí.* Maybe. Who knows,' Tomás said with a nod, clearly not really believing it.

The sun flashed on the deceitfully placid sea like a vast emerald. They made their way down the lonely promontory for their last, highly exceptional journey.

✳   ✳✳

The palm-stump idol with its two grimacing faces,

their talisman, was lashed to a stake at the front of the raft. They spent most of their days trawling with their inadequately-sized nets—they barely caught enough to supplement their supplies, but if they had fished any less they would have caught nothing. By night, to help keep them from getting lost or straying from the current, Tom taught Mike to navigate by the stars.

'Those two—at the edge of Ursa Major—'

'The Big Dipper,' mouthed Mike obnoxiously.

'Anyway, they point right to Polaris. This close to the Equator, it stays relatively close to the horizon, which makes it easier to pick out the points of the compass.' He pointed southwards. 'See that sort of twisting line of brighter stars, with a hint of the Milky Way behind it? That's Scorpio.'

'Hey, Sagittarius is next to Scorpio, right? That's me. Show me Sagittarius.'

Tom rolled his eyes, but gestured at a point further along the dimly luminous arm of the galaxy. 'There. *Claro*. See?'

'I don't see anything. I mean, I see a bunch of stars, but not a shape.'

With a smile and a shake of the head, Tom got behind his friend, took his finger, and traced the teapot shape of Sagittarius in front of both of them. 'Wow,' said Mike. 'That … does not look like a centaur at all.'

'Take it up with Hipparchus, *compañero*.'

'Huh?'

'Never mind.'

✳   ✳✳

After three weeks at sea, they had not made it quite as far (judging by the stars) as Mike had hoped; all the same, the weather had remained surprisingly mild, even for the end of summer. The air was warm, and the blue, glittering, sterile expanse of water around them was almost perfectly flat. The highest peaks of California's mountains had sunk with finality under the horizon some days before. Tom's olive skin had darkened to bronze, while Mike had been burned pink as a shrimp and then peeled like one.

'Oh my god the ocean sucks,' Mike said.

'Already said that today,' Tom said.

'Then the ocean is stupid.'

'Already said that too.'

'Then you're stupid.'

'Are you done?'

Mike rolled over onto his side, maybe to find a better vantage point from which to sulk. 'Wanna play *I Spy*?' he mumbled.

'*Sí, compañero*, I want to play *I Spy*. Here, in the middle of the Pacific. I'll go first. I spy with my little eye, the ocean. And I'll go second: I spy with my little eye, the sky. And there is not one single other thing to see, *¡cabrón!*'

'Yeesh. Sorry. Just trying to lighten the mood a little, broseph.'

Tom rolled his eyes and muttered a long string of oaths under his breath.

* **

Day followed day. They might have lost count, if not for the fact that there was so little else to do. Miraculously they hadn't lost anything, with the exception of one bag of walnuts dropped over the side by mistake. They didn't dare sleep through the whole night at the same time; when Mike was asleep, Tom would watch the glimmering stars of the southern hemisphere creeping toward them, and vice versa.

One morning, it began to rain. Tom had been about to waken Mike, but the cold spray spared him the trouble. He scowled and sat up with a dog-like shake of the head.

'Not funny, *hermano*. It can't be time to switch shifts yet.'

'It absolutely is. In fact I let you sleep in an extra half hour.'

'But it's so dark.'

Tom shrugged. 'It's overcast. The rain's back.'

His friend looked out to the horizon, and his face turned salt-white. 'We're fucked,' he said.

'What? *¿Por que?*'

'That's not rain,' Mike said, pointing to the southeast. 'That is a fucking cyclone.'

They stared at the oily clouds in the distance. A slow heave of the ocean beneath them signalled the beginning. Deceitfully gentle billows lowered and lifted them, and dots of rain spattered on their heads. The breeze, which had been mild and cool, grew stronger.

Tom snapped out of it first. '*Dio'nosalve*. It is just possible we can survive this.' He yanked the leather cord holding his cross as tightly as it would go around his throat, so that it wouldn't swing around. 'We have to strap down everything except ourselves right now.'

'How the hell can—'

'Strap everything the *fuck* down! Now!' He was already uncoiling rope and tossing it toward Mike. 'It might work, and nothing else can. *¡Te move!*'

They used all the rope they had. Thankfully their supplies were much lower now than they had been when they set out. The rain had thickened and gotten ice-cold before they finished, and a single earsplitting crack of thunder sounded above them as they were tying the final knots. A wave broke over them at almost the same moment, and would have swept one of their containers of fresh water right off the raft if Mike hadn't grabbed it in time. When the wave had slipped back off the raft, Tom rushed over to the mast and let in the sail, wrapping it tightly with its cords and knotting them securely at the bottom, and then throwing himself back down onto his stomach.

'Right,' Mike shouted over the sloshing of seawater, 'now what?'

'Now we cling to the raft like grim death and pray it doesn't capsize!'

'Seriously? *That's* your fucking plan? Like, *all* of it?'

'No! If it *does* capsize, get onto the bottom and cling to that!'

'Oh, brilliant!'

'This trip wasn't my fucking idea, *¡pendejo!*'

'No, you wanted to stay in Monterey till we both starved rather than take a risk!'

'Well here's the goddam risk you wanted, *"hermano,"* so don't whine at—'

At that moment a gigantic grey wave collapsed on top of them, and for several long moments everything was freezing water and the foul tang of seaweed in their mouths. As the raft heaved to the surface again, another stroke of lightning shot overhead, and then a thunderclap like a shattering door. Mike found his fingers still clinging to the raft, which hadn't even capsized. He looked to his right to yell at Tom.

Tom wasn't there.

Mike crawled to the edge of the raft, screaming his friend's name. He looked as far as he could, wiping rainwater out of his eyes. There was no sign of him anywhere. Once Mike thought he saw a figure, a good way off: it seemed to be a person, standing erect in the sea, with long dark hair lashing around their face; but then a giant blue-black wall rose in front of his eyes and threw itself over him.

✳ ✳✳

Slowly, with heat and a deep, reddish light pressing against his eyelids, Mike came to. Whatever was underneath him was not soft, exactly, but it was yielding. Sand. That's what it was. The sound of surf met his ears, now gentle and rhythmical. Cool wavelets tickled his feet. A bird chirruped somewhere close by. He rolled over with a groan, pushed himself onto his knees and palms, and opened his eyes.

The sand underneath him was jet black, but it still occasionally sparked in the powerful sun and hurt his eyes. Mike blinked a few times, trying to adjust. Leaning backwards into a kneeling posture, he looked around: a small expanse of beach, bordered by two big outcroppings of volcanic rock, lay between the ocean and a forest of Hawaiian myrtle and bamboo, with smaller shrubs and vines forming a thickly populated undergrowth. There were a few coconut palms leaning drunkenly out toward the beach as well. Some of the wreckage of the raft had washed up too, about forty yards to his right. The sky overhead was a clear, heartless blue. He'd made it. Alone.

The young man heaved himself to his feet. He was dully surprised that his clothes, while caked with salt and sand, had more or less survived the cyclone. Trudging over to what was left of the raft, he rummaged for any supplies that had not been swept off into the sea. A gallon of water, a big bag of pemmican, and a small one of dried apricots. The palm-stump idol had apparently cracked in half: only the face of Kanē had arrived with him. It looked like the rest of the wreckage and supplies were gone, but the hum of insects and the fluting of birds made it clear the island was healthy. He could forage while he hunted for Tom.

There was nothing to carry supplies in, so Mike set up shop on the beach for the day. Gathering driftwood and building a firepit was simple enough; getting it lit was more of a chore, but he'd been an avid camper before everything went to hell, and he managed. Once he had a small blaze going, he climbed up onto the larger outcropping, off to the right as he faced the interior of the island, to get a sense of the local geography.

It was the big island, he was pretty sure. The sun was still fairly low in the sky, so he could work out the points of the compass, and there was nothing on the eastern horizon but ocean. The island rose in rich green slopes on the other side, culminating in a distant black peak that had to be Mauna Loa, standing westward and a little south. The coast ran out to the northeast a little way and then curved back, perhaps two miles off. On the far side of the other outcropping, an irregular little bay was bitten into the coastline, followed by a slight bulge eastward, crowded with trees that blocked his view of most of the rest of the shore. In the offing he could just distinguish a few more stretches of beach.

He climbed down, with a final four-foot jump into the sand, and trudged back over to the fire. He opened the bag of pemmican and ate a few pieces. Tom was a good swimmer. It'd be a chore to find him among the scattered islands, but he would manage. If he'd survived the cyclone himself, there was no way Tom hadn't made it too.

The next few days were spent hunting through the nearer stretches of the forest for edible fruits and nuts. He unexpectedly found an unguarded quail's nest on the second day, and took half a dozen eggs, leaving five. On the third, a Dungeness crab was trapped in a tidal pool in one of the rocks on the shore. Occasional windfalls of this kind notwithstanding, he ran low on food quickly.

On the fifth day he saw something glinting in the morning sun on the beach. It wasn't the sand; the sand here was volcanic black, and whatever was flashing in the sunlight was pale. The little stretch of shore had become familiar enough that he felt sure this must have washed up in the night. He plodded over through the gently rising waves to pick it up.

He pulled it out of the sand. A thin leather cord, from which there hung a familiar gold cross.

A huge, horrible gap formed in Mike's chest, bloating outwards through his lungs and stomach. He clutched the cross till the metal arms almost punctured his skin. Tears came: rising with a sickening slowness over the brim, they made their tickling way down his cheeks into his beard. More came, and more. He wanted to howl, but no voice would come out of his mouth. Breath escaped, but sound fell, strangling and helpless, down into the darkness of his throat. He fell jerkily into a sitting posture, his mouth hanging open as he cried, and the waves sloshed over his legs, an alternating rhythm of rush and hiss, as if they were repeating over and over: *plash*—death; *plash*—death; *plash*—death; *plash*—death ...

✶ ✶✶

The following dawn, Mike gathered up every useful thing he could scavenge, made a rough knapsack out of the remains of the sail, selected a sturdy bamboo stalk from the floor of the forest, and began heading up the mountain. The forest wasn't quite as food-rich as he had hoped, but it would serve, and it was a hell of a lot more plentiful than the beach.

The trek up the mountainside was taxing. It was humid. Though the trees grew thickly overhead, the sun seemed to force its way through the leaves. Green heat wavered in the air in front of him and behind. He savored the effort, the ache in his legs, the blister forming on his right foot, the sweat on his throat and in his eyes and mouth. Nothing distracts from pain like pain.

A little past midmorning, Mike cleared the treeline. The upper half of the mountain was covered in expired volcanic flows, recent enough to be mostly free of vegetation; a fine breeze was blowing, so that, though it was still hot, the air was not nearly as stifling. He pushed himself forward. He was a small brown dot, moving along the border of the black expanse of stone beneath him and the limitless blue sky above.

When noon came, he had reached a lower crest of the mountain, and he sat down and ate some pemmican and dried mango. Over Mauna Loa's sloping right shoulder, he could see Mauna Kea further off. He decided to turn a little further east, rather than attempt to summit the mountains on a modest food supply, and stick close to the birds, fruits, and nectar-filled flowers that the Hawaiian forest afforded.

He wore away the rest of the daylight hiking, mostly in silence. There was a moment late in the afternoon, though, when the sun was lying across the volcanoes in golden and white and coppery bands, when Mike decided to sing. He wasn't much of a singer himself—at least, he'd never thought so, although Marina had always told him he had a better voice than he believed. The song that came to him was one that she had loved, and that Tomás had loved too; it felt good to sing it, there on the mountain, in the last dying hours of the summer.

> 'Yo fui a mi campo
> y encontré
> una rosita blanco
> crecend' ahí;
> esa flor bella mí
> alegría
> dio más mucho que

primer amor.
Cuando se marchita,
todavía
da rosit' aroma
sin reserva:
es' ensangrentado
aún bella ...'

But his voice wavered and fell there in the middle of the second verse, and he couldn't bring himself to sing any more. It only made the gap that he was feeling ache worse. He had always found it easy to look ahead, acknowledge losses, and move on. Marina had been the hardest to let go of, but he'd had people to fall back on then, like his parents or his sister or Tomás. He'd never faced any challenge completely alone.

When the sun set, darkness followed rapidly. He found a reasonably level patch of ground just outside the jungle (not actually in it, to help avoid insects), layered a good thick patch of palm leaves on top of it, and laid himself down to sleep. The stars whirled overhead, bright and hateful.

* **

The following day, he continued his march northward, staying more or less at the same elevation, tropical forest on his right and dried volcanic slag at his left. It felt a little strange to just drop the plastic bags that had contained his breakfast on the ground: but, for a change, his own littering really wouldn't make a difference any more. And it wasn't as if there were garbagemen now, even if it would have.

Most of the day was taken up traversing the fairly steep valley that separated the spur of Mauna Loa from the slightly lower sides of Mauna Kea. Five miles as the crow flies to every eight of actual effort was probably a generous estimate, he thought. But it was still marginally shorter than simply following the coast. And if Hawaii did happen to preserve any survivors—

Then they'd probably be on the coast. Both because that's where most settlements were in Hawaii anyway, and because the coast allowed for both foraging and fishing. How could he have been so stupid? He turned immediately to his right, to begin muscling back down to the beach through the jungle, and stopped in his tracks.

In front of him was a naked woman. No, not naked: she was wearing a sarong, which he hadn't registered at first because its colors were so like those of her skin, and her blue-black hair lay modestly over her breasts. Her eyes were a dark shade of brown, almost black, and a garland of white orchids sat on her head like a crown. She was smiling a curious smile: not smug or mocking or cunning, but in some way knowing; as if she had discovered something she expected, and important. Mike would probably have found her very attractive, all else being equal, but he was both too exhausted and too wired for that. He felt a vague *déjà vu* about her appearance.

'*Aloha Mikala,*' she said, and extended her hand.

Mike took it, hesitantly, and whispered, 'Thank you?'

She laughed brightly, and said something else he couldn't understand, but her expressions and gestures clearly meant something to the effect of *Follow me.* He did.

She led him east, toward the shore. There was a little less than an hour of day left, and when they came to the ruins of a small bayside town, it was sunset. They passed over cracked asphalt and concrete among silent, hollow buildings and wrecked cars, and came to a small inlet that twisted a little way into the city. A pair of men were standing on its beach, each one with a gigantic circular object tied to his back, which, when they were close enough to see, proved to be large but lightly built coracles. Both men were heavily tattooed, in patterns that seemed familiar, though Mike was too tired to think where he had seen them before. One had the shape of a large squid wrapped across his chest and a grid-like pattern on his forehead rather like the scaly skin of a pineapple, while the other sported large triangular patches around his eyes and a complicated, geometric sun disc on one shoulder.

'Hello,' Mike rasped. The men nodded, and spoke a little in Hawaiian to the woman who answered still more briefly. They untied their coracles from their backs, and one of the men gestured to Mike and then to his vessel, while the second man and the woman got into the other. Mike hesitantly got in—what else could he do?—and the man climbed in behind him. The woman's voice said, '*Hele.*' Without any apparent propulsion, whether mechanical or from the passengers, the coracles began to glide swiftly over the water and out northward into the bay. The warm, still air became a breeze as they sailed through it. They passed a moss-grey sea turtle burying her clutch of eggs on the beach. Within a few minutes they were on the open ocean, turning again, this time toward the faint crimson blush of sunset and the further archipelago. Mike wondered if he were dreaming.

✶ ✶✶

He must have nodded at some point, because suddenly he found himself being gently shaken awake and helped to disembark. It was still night, and he couldn't have been asleep for long, as the waning gibbous moon was still fairly low in the sky. He looked at the black mass of island in front of him. To his surprise, there was a distinctly marked path in the jungle, which was not only thoroughly cleared but lined with small torches. *Like a resort*, Mike thought, feeling idiotic. 'Where are we?' he asked, still unsure whether any of his companions spoke English. One of the men said, maybe in reply, '*O kēia Hikina Moloka'i.*'

The three of them began walking up the path; Mike followed. They walked for perhaps an hour, uphill, before they came to a large opening in the trees—not a volcanic scar, but a methodically cleared space, lined with stones and torches at the edge and with a small bonfire in the center. There were a few more people moving around the space, perhaps a dozen, all dressed in brightly dyed skirts and sarongs. Near the far side of the clearing and a little to the left was a large table, covered in banana leaves and groaning with fruit, seafood, and what looked like large wooden pitchers, though no one seemed to be eating or drinking. Directly to the right were two huts.

'*Aloha ahiahi,*' called the woman who had first greeted Mike. ''*Ane'i ka kekahi kanaka.*'

'*Kekahi kanaka? Aloha 'ino!*' answered one of the men in the clearing with a broad grin, and everyone laughed.

'*Hele ki'i ka mea mua kekahi,*' the woman said, this time to a specific person, a young woman in a turquoise skirt. ''*Ae, Wahine Poli'ahu,*' the other said in reply. She left the wide circle of firelight and went inside one of the huts. Mike's guide gestured graciously to the table and said, '*Ai*'; she seemed to be telling him to help himself. He went over to it, a little hesitantly—he *was* extremely hungry—and picked up a big chunk of pineapple. Glancing back at his guide, he saw her laugh again and pantomime eating.

He bit into the fruit. It was cold and sweet and sharp, like the shock of water when you cannonball into a pool on a hot day. He finished it, and ate another piece, and then a piece of what looked like roasted tuna still hot from the fire, beautifully oily and just a little bit singed at the edges. He picked up one of the jugs and took a swig from it: coconut water, which he'd never liked before, but he was so thirsty it didn't matter. He picked up a piece of starfruit and bit into its tart flesh.

'*¡Puta madre!* Mike!'

He turned around. Tom was running at him from the direction of the huts. He had seized him in a strangling hug before Mike could process what was happening.

The starfruit fell to the ground, and Mike started crying again, shamelessly and messily and with loud howls. His voice was back. He didn't really remember anything else that happened that night. There was crying, and hugging, and then a dim space with a large soft thing in it that felt wonderful to lie down on; and after a little while, the sound of rain.

Hours later, Mike's eyes drifted their way open, deliciously unhurried. It felt like a morning at the beginning of a vacation.

'Wakey wakey,' said a familiar voice.

'Tom,' he mumbled happily.

'In the flesh.'

'So I'm not still dreaming?'

'Not at this hour, it's almost noon.' He chuckled. 'Here, eat something.'

Mike sat up, and Tom thrust a bowl of assorted fruits

into his hands. He started in on a papaya. 'What in the hell happened to you? I thought you'd drowned. How did you get here?'

'I thought *you'd* drowned. That cyclone was … *pinche*. Anyway, when that giant wave hit the raft—did she capsize, by the way?'

'Nope.'

Tom nodded proudly. 'But when the wave hit, I felt something.'

'Yeah, a fuck-ton of water.'

'No, besides that. I felt a bunch of hands. Grabbing me, lifting me off the raft and into the water.'

'Hands? Like, just hands? Were they attached to anyone?'

'I never saw who it was. Or what it was. They were. If you want the truth, I panicked and then passed out. When I came to, I was here, and the *isleños* were bringing me food.' He scratched his chin. 'I think.'

'The food's pretty undeniable, broseph.'

'No,' Tom chuckled, 'I mean I think they're *isleños*, you know, ethnic Hawaiians. I'm not sure.'

Mike opened his mouth to make fun, and then thought of the coracles that moved at a word and the strange, maybe-there, maybe-mirage figure he had seen during the cyclone. 'I'm not sure either.'

There was a great, whooping cry outside the hut. Tom leapt up and went out, Mike right behind him. The Hawaiians were dancing and leaping around the extinct bonfire, shouting in unison: '*Ke nui ke ali'i! Ke nui ke ali'i!*'

'You don't speak Hawaiian, do you?' Michael asked.

'I'm afraid not.'

Mike peered at the dancers. 'Look. Look at their feet.'

The movements were natural enough at first glance; but they seemed to be spending more time in the air than gravity should have allowed them. Their leaps didn't look vigorous, yet they went so high and stayed up so long, as though their movements were being governed by the rules of their dance in a way that overrode the rules of physics. Their faces shone. *"Āina pau! Moana pau! Lani pau! Pilikia pau! E komo mai, makua, akua!'*

Without warning, the western horizon, visible through the trees, erupted in a fury of gold. Mike's first thought was of a volcano, but there was no smoke, and it didn't even really look like lava—and it looked like it was coming from the horizon itself, or out of the ocean. The sun was dimmed in comparison to that colossal brightness at the edge of the world, as it rapidly stretched its shimmering fingers across the sky.

'*Mira*,' Tom breathed, nudging his friend's shoulder and pointing behind them. There too, to the east, were the same beams of radiance. It was as though the whole world were being painted in gold leaf, like the background of a Byzantine ikon. Luminosity and warmth and a smell like lilies washed over them from both directions.

Mike whispered back, 'Are we dead?'

THE LAST MUEZZIN

Jibril bin Idris woke suddenly. He was in a shaded place, though the sun was casting an evil glare over the roads and buildings around him. He sat up and wondered where his *Baba* was—he didn't see him. It was hardly like him to be away at this hour of the morning. Indeed, it was usually around this time that he would be reciting a story to Jibril to while away the time, drawn perhaps from the *Kitab al-Miraj* or the *Thousand Nights and a Night* or the *Hadith*. The boy hugged his legs sullenly.

There was a mechanical crackling in the distance, followed by a nasal drone that was punctuated by spitting and irregular silences. It was the recording of the *azan*, or what was left of the recording, playing from the minaret of the al-Bahr. Jibril automatically turned eastward and stooped, rubbing his hands and arms with sand to cleanse them; he raised his hands to his ears and obediently murmured, '*Alláhu akbar. Subhánakalláhumma, wa bihamdik, wa tabárakasmuk, wa ta'álá yadduk, wa lá iláha ghairuk. Achúdhu billáhi min aš šaithani rrayím. Bismilláh ar-Rahman ar-Rahím ...*'

The immemorial verses of *salat* flowed over the boy's cracking lips. A falcon looked downward at him from a heat-laden updraft, its beady eye searching for likely prey. No, not that thing; it was much too big; it would put up a fight.

'*... wa rahmatullah. Alláhu akbar. Alláhu akbar. Alláhu akbar,*' recited Jibril, his voice sinking to a parched whisper. He stood up, coughed, and looked around again. Still no sign of his father. He picked up the water skin, shook it to be sure it was empty, slung it over his back by the aging leather strap, and began trudging toward the river.

The silvery shape of the Nile curved through the silent remains of Dumyáth: the last city of Mašr, a wasteland divided by serpentine waters. By all rights the soil of the delta ought to have been fertile, but the layers of concrete and garbage that Dumyáth exuded had made sure there was no chance of that for a long time. Since the factories and markets had shut down, the water at least had slowly cleared itself. Jibril lowered the skin below the surface, and it bubbled and glugged as the water filled it.

He set the skin carefully on a large rock by the bank, and then splashed his hands and face in the water, shaking his head like a puppy. His thick black hair clung to his cheeks. He had asked *Baba* if they could move to the edge of the river, but he had answered no, that the crocodiles made it too dangerous. Mindful of the warning, the boy climbed out of the water once he felt refreshed, and slung the water skin back over his shoulders and trudged back.

As he walked, he noticed a glittering object at the cracked edge of the road. Curious, he went over to it. It was a *misbachah*, the string of beads upon which the devout recited the Ninety-Nine Beautiful Names of Allah. *Baba* was never parted from his, but this looked strikingly like it: the beads were fashioned out of a rare, olive-green type of amber, and the cord was of black silk. Jibril had never much liked the litany of names, as he could never remember them properly, but the feel of the cord against his fingers was strangely soothing.

He picked it up, and thumbed his way idly through the beads. The sixteenth was slightly chipped. A wave of cold went through his stomach; mechanically, he wrapped it around the water skin's strap in a slip-knot and continued walking. This was his father's *misbachah*, there could be no doubt. It wasn't like him to leave it behind. No matter what he was doing, he would pull it out of his pocket (if he had even stowed it away) and murmur *zikr* as he went. What could have prompted him to abandon it?

By the time Jibril reached their camp, the recording in the minaret was crackling and buzzing again. It was already time for the *Asr*. Using fresh water for the purification was out of the question, it was too precious; so, trying not to worry over *Baba* or resent the ruined pleasure of his bath, he knelt down and began to rub his arms and face with hot, coarse sand again.

'*Alláhu akbar. Subhánakalláhumma, wa bihamdik …*'

The *Maghrib* after sunset passed, and still *Baba* had not returned. Jibril was becoming terribly hungry. There was a red-throated loon not far off, mewing, as if it too were saying the *Maghrib*. The boy thought, and stood. There was only so long he could wait.

He slung the water skin back over his shoulders, took a step, and stopped: there was a stone in his shoe. He sat down on the ground to pull it out, then got up again and went out into the night to search.

It was surprisingly cool. Jibril sniffed the air; the dry smell of decaying stone mingled with reedy waftings from the river. He walked south, more or less following the river's course, though the tangled roads tried hard to divert him. He didn't call out for his *Baba*. There were wild animals in parts of the city, scavengers for the most part, but predatory enough that it was better not to draw their attention— hyænas, jackals. The moon rose as he walked into the outskirts of Dumyáth, a vague blot of light in the hazy air.

In the distance he saw a rumpled shape, heaving in the dark. A dying animal, maybe. As Jibril drew closer to it, it made a throaty noise as if it were trying to growl. He looked at it again. It was elongated, with a dull coat, apelike paws, and a much longer flow of hair at the head, like a mane. It didn't look exactly like a hyæna, it was too slender for that, and far too large for a monkey.

An ugly possibility came to him. He stopped in his tracks, a few meters away from the thing. Suddenly Jibril didn't want to know what it was, didn't want to hear it or see it at all any more. It wasn't *Baba*. It couldn't be. And since he needed to find *Baba* he was going to go away and do that. He turned away and kept on walking. His hands were shaking.

The fringe of the city receded behind him. Jibril's aching head seemed, sieve-like, to be draining of conscious thought, leaving behind only a film of sensations. The heaviness of sleep. The coarseness of sand underfoot. Thirst. Dimness. The smell of the river. Cold.

A bird's cry, melancholy and sweet, broke the silence. It was prolonged and complex, like a nightingale, but as deep as a mourning dove and with a strange, brassy timbre. It not only roused him, he was so struck by its beauty that he stopped to attend to it.

He had scarcely halted his progress when a shadow flew across the ghostly moon. Though there was no wind that night, there was a great rushing sound, as of some gigantic creature flying rapidly through the air. Jibril breathed slowly. He knew he was a good runner, but a creature with wings …

Something landed on the ground in front of him. He could not make it out clearly in the gloom, but it was a bird of some kind, colossal in size, built rather like an eagle but with an elongated neck. If Jibril had ever seen a swan he would have compared it to that, but he had not.

It regarded him silently. He did not move. Then the bird looked up, and the air stirred; a powerful wind must have been blowing, miles above, for suddenly the haze was ruffled and torn and finally blown right out of the skies, so that starlight and moonlight shone clearly on the desert floor.

The bird was one that the child had never seen before, even in pictures; but it sounded like the descriptions of the *eanqa'* that his father had told—he thrust that thought roughly away. The bird's plumage was satin, deep crimson in color, with a small golden crest rather like a peafowl, and a long, ibis-like beak. Its breast showed soft scarlet down paling into gold, while its wings and its voluminous tail darkened to purple at the tips. The bird's eyes were curiously bright. There was a sinuous line of vivid green among the feathers on its long throat, formed (it was impossible, but it was unmistakable) into *letters*:

وَسِعَ كُرْسِيُّهُ السَّمَوَاتِ وَالأَرْضَ

وَلاَ يَؤُودُهُ حِفْظُهُمَا

وَهُوَ الْعَلِيُّ الْعَظِيمُ

Words from the Throne Verse. The silence lengthened. Then, very deliberately, the bird bowed its head to him.

Jibril thought, and bowed in response.

The *eanqa'* could hardly smile with a beak, yet there was something in its demeanor that was pleased, or respectful, or kind. It fluted a few notes to him, and then began to walk eastward, away from the heart of the city.

'*La, tayir,*' Jibril burst out, unthinkingly. Animals would attack the bird on the ground, and it was his only company in his *Baba's*—absence; and besides, the bird was so beautiful that he did not like to think of its being attacked. But the bird simply turned and cooed to him, and began to walk again.

He hesitated and followed, hurrying to catch up.

✶ ✶✶

They walked that way all night. Once, Jibril stumbled, and the *eanqa'* drew closer to him and ruffled its wings in a peculiar way. It seemed to be inviting him to lean against it. Tentatively—it seemed presumptuous to touch the bird, yet even more presumptuous to reject its offer of help—Jibril put out a hand and rested it on the back of the *eanqa'*. The feathers were sleek and shimmered like a peacock's, yet they were soft to the touch. The bird made a whirring, contented sort of sound, and they continued to walk.

Around midnight, when the moon set, he realized he had forgotten to say the *Isha*. He paused; the bird paused with him. He did not want to pray. He was alone, thirsty, tired, and cold; and, if he was brutal with himself, he knew his *Baba* was not praying the *Isha* now. Conscience and passion struggled inside him; after about a minute, Jibril angrily flung himself into the sand, performing the ablutions and reciting the *rak'at* as quickly as possible, omitting the voluntary prayers his father had always added. The strange pair then proceeded; but Jibril thought coldly of verses from the *Qur'an* describing the *Miraj*, the night journey of the Prophet's ecstasy:

Subhánal lazé asrá bi'abdihé lailam minal Masyidil Harámi ilal Masyidil Aqsal-lazé bárakná haw lahó linuriyahó min áyátiná; inahó Huwas Sam'éul-Basér ... Fakána qába qawsaini aw adná. Fa awhá ilá 'abdihé má awhá: Holy is He who took His servant by night from the Sacred Mosque unto the Uttermost Mosque, the precincts of which We have blessed, that We might show him some of Our signs. Surely it is He who is the all-seeing, the all-hearing. ... This manifestation is now visible upon the spiritual horizons. That servant approached closer to Allah ... Jibril too was eager to approach Allah—eager to require a sign, a vision, an explanation. He gripped the *misbachah*, straining the cord.

Since Dumyáth lay in the Delta, it seemed impossible

that they should have walked so long without meeting one of the curling tendrils of the Nile; but they had not. The landscape about them was flat and bare, and the greyish-red sand of Mašr was abrading Jibril's feet. An orange line appeared in the eastern sky and increased slowly.

His drifting mind lit on the story of Iblis—the fallen spirit of fire, supreme among the *jinn*, who had refused Allah's command to bow to Adam. The mosque's *'ulamá* had often spoken of him, both before and during the collapse of the city; they always pointed to his hubris as the cause of his fall, urging the supreme necessity of unquestioning, instant obedience to the will of Allah, expressed in both the *Qur'an* and in the events of daily life, which man must not gainsay. Man must not gainsay; that was the heart of Islam; yet in the *Miraj*, the holy Musa had ordered the Prophet himself, the most surrendered of all Muslims, to haggle with Allah over the required prayers, and he had done so. Allah Himself had condescended to accede to the bargaining of Muhammad. And old Faruq, the *imam* of their mosque, had once told Jibril's father in his hearing that the *Súfiyún* who had educated him told a different story about the text concerning Iblis: that he gladly accepted hell, rather than bow to anyone or anything save Allah, so great was his love of his Creator.

The *eanqa'* had stopped. Jibril only realized it when his hand slid suddenly upward along its outstretched neck. He came out of his reverie to find the bird, and himself with it, standing atop a cliff. It extended its long, swanlike neck and uttered five notes, as sweet as silver bells yet with the force of trumpet-blasts. The boy shivered. The *eanqa'* became quiet, and the two waited.

A point of light appeared in the east; but it was not the sun. The dawn's light was showing, but that very illumination seemed grey beneath the piercing, terrible radiance that was now showing itself.

At first it was too far off for any color or shape to be distinguishable; but as it drew closer, it changed. A shape like an inverted teardrop was revealed, shimmering with iridescent purples and greens and silvers and blues. A voice from an unseen source, heavy as gold, thundered out: *'Aintahá al-Ghumud! Aqtarab al-Tawús Malak! Lamah, aqtarab al-Tawús Malak! Aqtarab mae šach-abah ešr't-alaf, aqtarab!' The Occultation is ended! Behold, the Peacock Angel approacheth! With ten thousand of his companions, the Peacock Angel approacheth, he approacheth!*

The *eanqa'* spread its wings and bowed with serpentine grace. Not knowing what else to do, Jibril put his hand on his breast and bowed his head. Slowly, the turquoise luminescence drew close to the bird and the boy, drowning out brown skin, grey earth, and crimson feathers in overwhelming light. He closed his eyes, but still the brilliance came through.

The great voice spoke again: *'Al-Munkar w' al-Nakir, al-Málik w' ar-Rizwan, Kiraman Katibin w' Mu'aqqibat: alhamdulillah, ar-Rahman, ar-Rahím; aqtarab al-abdullah al-Tawús Malak ar-rasulan.'* 'The Peacock Angel approaches the prophet'? What prophet? But the radiance was becoming so unbearable that he could hardly think.

The boy felt a many-fingered hand on his chin, and someone told him to open his eyes. Trembling a little, he did; and the world was unmade.

Jibril knew at once that he was not looking at Allah's face. This was only a herald—this kind of love, shining out of fire and in the form of fire, was unmistakably the adoring kind of love that is, before all else, directed upward. All the same, if the very heralds looked like this, he wondered for a fleeting moment whether he would live through the preparatory stages of the vision.

✳   ✳✳

As the sun was sinking the following evening, Jibril's bare feet pounded against the sand at the outskirts of the city of Dumyáth as he ran. He heard the recording of the *azan* crackle to life, then slow down, become distorted, gutter, and die; the power had run out at last. He laughed.

Far away to his right, there was the dark, irregular lump. The reddening light showed it plainly to be his *Baba*'s body. He didn't stop.

Cracked roads, piles of trash, little rivulets, and scavenging insects flew by him as he found his way to the Mosque of Amr. He glanced westward: still a minute or so till sundown. There was the great northern minaret. He kicked the door in (the lock had rusted almost to nothing) and raced up the spiral staircase, careless of his own dizziness. The joy in him was too deep, too powerful, he had to get some of it out.

The door at the top of the staircase banged against the white stone wall as Jibril shot out, catching himself at the waist-high barrier among the arches. The sun was just touching the horizon, its brilliance dimmed by the haze to the color of a burning coal. Above it shimmered the evening star; it was lonely in the sky, pearlescent against the red-and-grey plumage of the sunset. It was time for the last *Maghrib*. Jibril laughed for joy and jumped up and down as he cried out at the top of his lungs.

'*Alláhu akbar! Alláhu akbar! Alláhu akbar! Alláhu akbar! Alláhu akbar! Alláhu akbar!*'

HIPPODAMUS

The branches broke easily, and the scent of the wood was pleasing. It was nice to think that, allowing for the circumstances, this would be a dignified death.

There weren't many olive trees left; but, even if that did matter to the gods, the man vaguely supposed that they could make more if they wanted them. Always assuming that the gods did not depend on humans to exist: that never had been settled, and probably couldn't be, by men. Except perhaps in Hades itself. He cracked the branch he was holding in two, and then split the pieces, stacking them carefully around his makeshift divan. It was no more than a few large stones covered in moss and flowers, over which he had laid a doe-skin, but it was comfortable and even beautiful.

One of the crows fluttered down onto the stump of one of the olive trees, looking around at the toiling man and his large, curious nest. It croaked interrogatively at him. The man did not reply, and the crow looked down at the ground and spotted some broken walnut fragments. It hopped down and began to snatch them up greedily.

The man had decided only that morning. It was amazing how simple loneliness made things. In the old days, making a choice so momentous—no; that was it; choices weren't momentous any more. There was nothing left for them to be momentous *about*.

✳   ✳ ✳

When he had moved out to the area after his wife's death, two years before, he had had one companion, their daughter Helene. Both devout practitioners of pagan ways, he and his wife had named her in honor of the ancient princess, for whose divine beauty the Greeks had conquered Troy. Never a strong child, Helene too had died, four months ago. He had built her a pyre and then collected her ashes, burying them at the foot of the great terebinth tree she had loved. After that, he had made the trek to Dardanellia—*Çanakkale*, the inhabitants used to insist on calling it, but the man was born a Greek and he would die a Greek—to visit his mother and bring her the unhappy news.

When he arrived, clothes for a few days' worth of family mourning stowed in his knapsack, the city was utterly silent. He went to his mother's apartment, but found it empty. He tried her best friend, her sister, the priest of her parish; all were absent. The houses and the shops were shut up, the offices and agency buildings dark. A damp breeze from the Ægean whispered between the buildings. Admittedly Dardanellia was not what it used to be, but this kind of total stillness was unnatural. He rubbed his hands together, blowing on the tips of his fingers, and went to check his mother's parish.

The Church of the Seven Sleepers was octagonal in shape, built out of pale, yellowish stones and topped by a tiled dome. Its western lintel, between the two chief doors, bore carved words.

Ο ΟΙΚΟΣ Ο ΘΕΟΥ

ΚΑΙ ΙΗΣΟΥ ΧΡΙΣΤΟΥ ΥΙΟΥ ΑΥΤΟΥ

ΣΥΝ ΤΟΙΣ ΑΓΙΟΙΣ ΕΠΤΑ ΚΕΚΟΙΜΩΜΕΝΟΙΣ

Below that was a mosaic depicting the saints it commemorated, the seven men who (legend said) had been marked for death by the Emperor Decius, but had fallen asleep in a cave and remained there two hundred years, until they awoke in a Christian empire and gave miraculous proof of the resurrection to the populace: Maximilian, Iamblichus, Martinian, John, Dionysius, Constantine, and Antoninus. Christ sat enthroned above them, the Mother of God on one side and the Archangel Jegudiel with a trumpet on the other. The church's two porticoes were set at angles to the *ikonostasis*, so that on entering, one would have to turn and reorient oneself.

The man's mother had explained it once, something about the otherworldliness of the sacred, but he hadn't really listened. He had always been a pagan at heart.

He pushed a door open. The temple interior, crowded with gold and blue depictions of the Christians' heavenly beings, was uncharacteristically dark: ordinarily there would be a few dozen candles burning before the icons at any given time. It was also chilly, and the smell of old incense was overpowering, as if every thurible had been filled to the brim and set alight at once. In fact, it was so distracting that at first, he didn't notice that the church was full of people.

They were not standing, as he would have expected, but seated in the *stakidia* along the walls, apparently fast asleep. A bishop was there—he didn't know which one —reclining in state on his throne at the side of the church: the figured silk of the *sakkos* and the *ômoforion* glittered even in the darkness up to his thick, snowy beard, and the cross-crowned *mitra* on his head flashed with gold, rubies, and enameled icons. He had all the gilt majesty of an emperor. Despite the newcomer, no one moved or spoke.

Bewildered, the man approached one of the laymen in the *stakidia*. It was a woman about his own age, apparently in the military, since she was dressed in its official drab. More mysteriously, she wore a silver crown, somewhat in the style of a nuptial crown, with a white velvet cap beneath the arches and a row of alternating sardonyxes and pearls along the circlet. In her right hand was an old-fashioned, metal crucifix in low relief, with the words Ὁ Βασιλεύς τῆς Δόξης incised into the top bar.

'*Chaire?*' he said to her quietly. '*Mboreis na me akouseis, kyria?*'

There was no reply. He tried again, a little louder. Nothing. He walked around the *stakidia* and even up to the bishop's throne, trying to rouse people, but no one woke. It was at this point that he noticed the smell.

It wasn't the smell of the incense, which he had finally been in the church long enough for his senses to ignore. It was something else, strange for this place, but also familiar in its way. Not a church smell. It made him think of bathrooms and laundries, for some reason: an astringent, medical kind of odor. Bleach, that was it.

An ice-cold pulse went through him. Chlorine gas. The incense was meant to mask the smell while they waited.

The man flew out of the shrine filled with mummies and ran up the street blindly. Empty buildings flashed past him. He didn't know how long he ran, but when he finally halted on a bridge over the river, gasping for breath, the shadows were markedly longer than they had been when he first reached the city. He stared into the water, sweating, unable to stop imagining the waxlike faces in the church. His stomach twisted; he leaned over the railing and vomited. There was an ugly splash, and the river swept it away as if it had never been.

*　**

He couldn't go back and look for his mother. She was surely in some church or other, undecaying, quietly being chemically transfigured, slowly; the mere thought of searching made him shudder. He spent another few days in the city, hardly eating, telling himself he was looking for survivors—but he didn't really fool himself. The problem was that there was little more purpose to leaving than to staying; any action took an inordinate amount of effort.

After a while, the man went to the city museum. A stray light bulb told him it still had power, somehow. He broke one of the windows to get in; a klaxon-wail of an alarm met his ears. He found a computer in a small office in the rear of the building, turned it on, and began to look for help.

The e-mails he sent returned a curious set of error messages, and after about an hour he stopped trying. He went through his social sites—he hadn't bothered to deactivate them when he left home—and noticed that there had been no updates for over a week, anywhere, even among his international friends in Europe and America. Alarmed, he searched for news.

It was all at least several months old, and all disquieting. A bizarre black cloud over Jakarta, thought to be the product of a volcanic eruption (though none had been recorded), had blotted out the sun, and the toxic gases released by it had suffocated everyone in the city. A plague had decimated northern India, from Kolkata to Mumbai, with symptoms corresponding to no disease known to medical history. Abrupt, unaccountable, absolute silence from Madrid, which neither journalists nor official personnel had yet been brave enough to investigate in person. Riots in Tokyo, prompted by no discernible cause, causing a mass exodus that had reduced the world's most crowded metropolis to a ghost town of a few hundred. And over and over, word of gigantic cities that were literally smoking craters for reasons unknown. Paris: gone. Seoul: gone. São Paulo: gone. Nairobi: gone. Shanghai: gone.

✳ ✳✳

He had lingered uselessly in the city for a few days more after that, until the nightmares finally gave him a reason to move. He kept dreaming that he was back in the ghastly Church of the Seven Sleepers, looking around and around at the crowned and lovely dead, and that the doors of the church had vanished. At first, he could ignore it on waking; but then it began to add the detail that he knew, with the intuition of dreams, that the suicides were only pretending to be dead, and at any moment, one of them would open its horrible eyes and look him in the face, and then he would able to do nothing but scream and scream.

He went to the city library and hunted for some books. He didn't know what he meant to do later on, but at any rate he wanted something to occupy himself with until he decided. There wasn't as much room in his knapsack as he would have liked, but it wasn't as though the library were at risk of being looted; struck by lightning, perhaps, yet it was made of stone. The man had usually preferred light, humorous works, but at this juncture, he found he gravitated toward the great books of the world. It took him some time to decide. The *Iliad*. Æschylus' plays. The *Bhagavad Gita*, since the whole *Mahabharata* would be too heavy. The complete works of Aristotle. The Bible. Suetonius' *Twelve Cæsars?* No, not enough room. *The Romance of the Three Kingdoms*. The *Daodejing* of Laozi. The *Kebra Nagast* of the kings of Abyssinia. The *Lotus Sutra*. The Quran. The Latin hymns of Venantius Fortunatus. A slender, nearly new copy of *Diwan-e-Hafez*. A French version of the *Epic of Sundiata*. *Tsurezuregusa*, in Japanese and English. He reached for a Greek version of *Le Morte D'Arthur*, thought, and then took the shorter *Othello* instead. The complete plays of Aleksandr Pushkin. Kierkegaard's *Fear and Trembling*. *El Libro de Arena* by Borges. Kazantzakis' inimitable *The Last Temptation of Christ*. He had to throw out his spare pair of shoes to fit the last five volumes, but he couldn't bear to take fewer.

On his way out of the city, he broke into a hospital and took a bottle of morphia. Hopefully it would help him sleep more soundly while he decided what to do.

The man walked slowly once he was clear of Dardanellia. It took six and a half hours to get back. The sea crashed against the rocks to his right, unmoved. He hardly saw where he was going, but when he glanced up occasionally, he noticed that the clouds had a glowering, oily look. He wondered vaguely whether that same venom that had devastated the trailing islands of Indonesia had been swept northwest by the wind.

He had been living near Hisarlik, as close as possible to the old site of Troy. It hadn't been romanticism that had drawn him there when he left home; it had just felt right when he stopped. Besides, Helene had liked the place. The man got back to his hut and sat in the doorway, staring unthinkingly at the wooden frame.

✻ ✻✻

It took him three months to work through the books he had taken. There was little else to do, except scavenge for food and walk around. Several of them were quite difficult to understand, but he had a burning need to finish them. A few times he tried to articulate to himself why this, of all things, should feel urgent, but he never lingered over the problem for more than a minute or so before the itch overcame him again.

Then one day, very late in summer, the man closed *The Last Temptation*. He thought about going back to Dardanellia and getting more; but the idea of returning to that ghastly city, where the dead were not dead but waiting, to open their fatal eyes on him and—he shook himself. It was a dream, only a dream. It wasn't real. All the same, he couldn't go back there.

It was then that he had to face the fact that (he now realized) his mind had been trying to protect him from. There was, quite literally, nothing to do.

He had tried to go on for a while after that. He reminded himself that he didn't actually know that he was the last. He thought of what his daughter or his wife would have said, had they been there. He recited passages from the classics to himself, on men's responsibility to each other and to the gods to remain at the post of life until dismissed. Three more weeks passed, and the days grew slowly briefer and more cold.

That morning the man had woken up and, very simply, realized what he would do. He wasn't sure he wanted to do it exactly; he just knew that he would. He remembered the morphia, which he hadn't touched since getting back: some submerged part of him had known what he was actually taking it for. Lying on his pallet with his eyes closed, he quoted to himself from an old story he'd read somewhere, '*O chaos anichnevsi … Eimai o televtaios … Tha po sto keno akroasi …*'

He had taken the hut to pieces for the pyre, but there had not been enough wood, so he cut down one of the olive trees as well. Then he took each of the books and carefully arranged them atop the wood, each one's upper edge pointing toward the land of its origin, as best he could manage. He had some pitch left over from when he first built his hut—on days when it was too wet to get the fire going, he had used it for that purpose. He poured it around the edges, to help make sure that the flames would be hot and smothering enough.

As he finished, he gazed upwards. Though it was still early in the evening, the sky was curiously dark. Storm clouds were huddling around the remains of the empty cities.

He bent down to light the fire, but something felt strangely unfinished about the work and he stopped, thinking. Then he went back to where the hut had been and rummaged among his stores until found a single pomegranate, and placed it among the broken pieces of wood, to honor Persephone, queen of the dead.

As if in answer, there suddenly shone a deep, fiery, golden light. He looked up again, and saw that the setting sun had come low enough to break through the clouds in the west. Smiling faintly, he climbed over his handiwork onto the makeshift divan. He set the fire in the pitch in two or three places and whispered, '*Erchomai, charitômenai.*'

He sat for a few moments, smelling the smoke; it had not yet grown choking. The crow hopped a little closer, tilting its head at him quizzically. After a few moments' study, it cawed a farewell and flapped away.

The man picked up the little bottle, opened it, drank it, and lay himself down on the divan, listening to the slowly rising cracks and hisses of the fire. The heat was becoming uncomfortable, but the smell of olive wood and resin and myrrh curled over him like the arms of a lover. The northern clouds were rumbling in the half-light, and the bright copper of the moon, opposite the fading sunset, lit the storm too with fire.

He spoke. '*Hôs hoi amfieton tafon Hektoros hippodamoio.*' The wind rose.

THE UNOFFENDING FEET

The earth lay silent. The sun stood at the zenith over Hawaii; the ruined shrines of Kyoto saluted their last dawn; the Andes and the Appalachians were preparing for a final sunset. In Jerusalem, it was midnight, and it should have been dark.

It was not. Over two of the last faces, a strange light —not like the deathly luminosity of bombs, but heavy with a golden and terrible life—was coming out of the sky. It fell on the softened summit of a mountain close to the city, and the air rustled the branches of the olive trees like a multitude of wings. Something dappled-white and slender and brilliant was coming out of the sky. The ground shook.

Suddenly, there was a roar of noise, louder than the loudest thunder, but with a different quality: musical, like trumpets, yet full of the warmth and vitality of voices. The soles of a pair of feet, marked with perforating crimson wounds, set themselves upon the mountaintop.

ABOUT THE AUTHOR

Gabriel Blanchard has been published in *Crisis* and *PRISM Magazine,* and is the author of the blog *Mudblood Catholic.* He writes prose fiction, poetry, personal and theological essays, and reviews, and is a regular contributor for Pints & Prose. He currently resides in Baltimore and has lived in California, Scotland, and Japan.

Black Velvet (The Erin O'Reilly Mysteries #1)

Steven Henry

When an art heist at the Queens Museum leaves an officer
down, Erin and her K9 partner face down criminals, art
dealers, and obstructive detectives in a race to capture the
killers—and maybe bring closure to a 75-year-old crime.

*"This book kept me going from start to finish...Can't wait to follow
more of their adventures!"*

"A must read! Love it!"

Learn more at clickworkspress.com/erin01.

Punishment: A Love Story

Eve Tushnet

A lesbian parolee re-integrates into life in DC in a dark comedy about the dangers and delights of humiliation.

"Another hilarious offering from Tushnet!"

"was happy to discover Punishment is similar to the author's previous work…often droll, but with an earnest heart."

Learn more at clickworkspress.com/punishment.